Assaie's Gift

Assaie's Gift

D E Howard

D E Howard

Second Edition September 2016

Edited by Lacy Lieffers (lacy.lieffers@oneleafediting.ca)
https://ca.linkedin.com/in/lacylieffers

Copyright © 2016 D E Howard

The moral right of the author has been asserted.

All rights reserved.
No part of this publication may be reproduced, stored in a retrieval system, or transmitted, in any form or by any means, without the prior permission in writing of the publisher, nor be otherwise circulated in any form of binding or cover other than that in which it is published and without a similar condition including this condition being imposed on the subsequent purchaser.

Typesetting services by BOOKOW.COM

Chapter One

"No, you can't do it... you just can't."

"I think I am too old for you to tell me what I can and can't do, don't you?"

"But this, you don't know the cost..."

"I know the cost if I don't."

"Why not just sleep on it? Give it some time and then see how you feel?"

"You think me foolish sister? I take a nap and before I know it a century has passed and it's too late."

"Maybe that would be for the best."

"Not for me. I love him; I have to be with him. I can't not. I'm sorry but I can't. He's my heart."

"He's just a man, a mortal man like any other..."

"No," Assaie smiled, her eyes sparkled as thoughts of the man she spoke of danced through her mind. "No, he is far more than that... he is... I don't know... he is everything."

Aalegth shook her head slowly, even as she argued with her younger sister she knew the argument was lost, and yet she could not give up without at least trying.

"Anfare talk some sense into our sister won't you?" Aalegth said, her words directed at the middle of the three sisters. "Stop her from making a huge mistake, she won't listen to me."

"Maybe Aalegth has a point," Anfare said with a gentle smile, "He is just a mortal man."

"But I love him," Assaie repeated. She may have been the youngest of the three but Assaie knew her heart and she was not about to be swayed.

"She does love him Aalegth," Anfare said with a shrug towards her eldest sister.

Aalegth couldn't keep the smile from playing on her lips, no matter what the situation you could always count on Anfare to sit on the fence, gladly seeing both sides of any argument and never able to fully support either one.

The three sisters looked at each other, in many ways mirror images of each other whilst at the same time being startlingly different. All three of them elegant and slender with silken locks that flowed below their shoulders and flawless ivory complexions with a hint of pink dusted on their cheeks.

Aalegth's golden hair shone with a brightness to rival the brightest sunny day, while Anfare's auburn hair glowed a fiery red and Assaie's ebony locks seemed to steal away the light and shine with its own special darkness.

Each sister was a beauty in their own right but the thing that would really have made someone take pause for a closer look was the intensity of their eyes. No word had yet to exist to describe them as they were never the same colour from one moment to the next. One minute they could be a dazzling blue only to have changed to a soft chocolatey hazel the next and an intense sea green a moment later. The strangeness of their eyes might have proved unusual and distracting in some but in the sisters it just added to their beauty, emphasising their uniqueness and their similarities, marking them out for what they were.

Three sisters. Three Goddesses.

The Goddesses had watched over the realms below them for countless centuries, loving their inhabitants and being loved in return. Asking for nothing but the love that was so freely given and rewarding it with a comfortable life for all those under their care.

So different than the Elder Gods who had tired of watching over their people.

For centuries the Elder Gods had amused themselves with the lives of the people on the world below, watching as they grew and developed, each new generation improving upon the knowledge and skills of their fathers.

Where once stood a shack made from sticks and mud surrounded by a scattering of random plantings now stood a sturdy stone farmhouse, its crops carefully sown in lines, planted and harvested along with the seasons. Where once the mortals would scrabble on the dirt to supplicate themselves before their gods, now stood churches with stone carvings of the deities to be worshipped upon a rough hewn stone altar stained red with the blood of the animals sacrificed to the Gods.

Now, the prayers that were once cried out to the heavens with heartfelt praise and longing had grown stale. Words were now said by rote, with little more meaning than if they were reciting a poem. The sacrifices, once the fattest and most valuable sheep, were now more often than not an elderly ewe no longer capable of lambing, or a sickly runt that would not make it to adulthood.

The Gods had grown bored, and mankind had grown complacent.

Looking down upon his realm the God Athego let out a snarl. He had allowed his people to grow fat and lazy, safe in their belief that their God loved them and would always protect them.

"No more!" Athego roared, slamming his fists down upon a table that glistened like diamonds crushed amidst fresh white snow. "It is time you learned the wrath of your God!"

At first the people of Athego were unaware of the anger of their God, they simply marvelled at their good fortune that had allowed the sun to shine a little longer and a little brighter this year. Then, as month after month passed with no rainfall, as crops began to wither and cattle die of thirst, the people raised their head to the heavens and prayed. They prayed as they had never prayed before, tearing at their clothes in supplication and offering sacrifices of what little livestock they had left, but it was to no avail. Athego did not relent.

When the people of the land began to starve, fearing that their God had forsaken them, they knew they had no other option but to travel to the lands ruled by the Goddess Sairah and beg for aid.

The people of Sairah were a kind and gentle people, and had only one or two of those in need come for aid it would have been given gladly and freely, but when the elders of the land saw the numbers that were crossing their borders they had no choice but to turn them away. While they did not wish to see Athego's people starve they knew that if they gave away their carefully harvested crops and their stores of grain then they too would soon be in need. And so they closed the gates and turned their heads from the cries for help, shedding tear for those who would surely die without it.

The people of Athego were in desperate need and, armed with weapons crudely fashioned from farmyard tools they attacked. Weakened as they were near starvation, desperation drove them on and soon the tracks were stained red with the blood of the fallen; the screams of Sairah's people echoed through the land.

Angered by what she was witnessing, Sairah stepped down from the heavens, raised her arms high above her head and vanquished the invaders in an instant, causing them to fall where they stood; life instantly extinguished.

Athego growled in anger that the Goddess should take such liberties with his people and he too laid his feet upon the earth. Stepping forwards ahead of the second wave of peoples from his lands Athego led the attack, laying waste to all mortal life that stood in his way. Snuffing out breath with a flick of his fingers and sending crashing bolts of lightening from a clear blue sky to lay waste to all of the buildings around him.

Sairah quickly retaliated, slaughtering without hesitation, matching Athego's fury blow for blow.

The battle raged on from day into night and all through the next day, neither God nor Goddess noticing for some time that no human life remained.

It was only when Sairah notice the red stain on her feet that she paused her actions, and looked upon the ground that was now littered with corpses. Those who had once worshipped her now lay dead at her feet. Sairah wept.

Athego saw the tears of the Goddess and he too looked around himself. He had been angered that his people had let their worship of him become a habit rather than a love, and now there were none of his people left to raise their head to him in prayer.

"What have we done?" Sairah asked, raising herself back into the heavens and away from the horror she had helped cause. "This can never happen again."

All of the Gods and Goddesses of the heavens had witnessed the slaughter in the lands of Sairah and Athego and were appalled, and yet in their hearts, each knew they would were capable of the same act.

So it was decreed that no deity should ever be allowed to walk the earth again in their true form. If they should ever wish their feet to touch the earth it would be in the body of a mortal, to live and die as any mortal would, only to ascend back into the heavens upon their passing.

All of this happened centuries before Assaie and her sisters ascended the heavens, the troubles seeming little more than stories to the Goddesses whose realm now lived in peace while the sisters watched over the people in their care.

Assaie had known that Jacob was special from the moment of his birth. Each new child gave the Goddess' cause to celebrate but he had been unique. To Assaie he was instantly something different to every other child born and, as he grew into a man, her interest in his life intensified. Assaie had felt a heart wrenching jealousy when she witnessed Jacob share his first kiss with a young woman in the village and eventually she had to admit that her feelings for him were not that of a Goddess, but of a woman. For him she wanted to be a woman, to be his woman.

"Your love might not be enough," Aalegth said gently, her fingertips brushing lightly over her sister's cheek. "What if he doesn't love you back?"

"Then he doesn't," Assaie said, her shoulders raising in a half shrug, "But I have to try, to know. Otherwise? No. No I can't spend eternity wondering what might have been."

"Then my beautiful sister, I wish you luck," Aalegth's eyes shone blue with tears. "I wish you luck and love and know that your sisters watch over you while you walk the earth."

The three sisters moved into an embrace; they had never been parted before and the thought gave them a moment's pause. Aalegth and Anfare knew their youngest sister's heart would always rule her head and once her heart was set on a path nothing could sway her. They just hoped that her heart would find its desire and not be irrevocably broken by the follies of a mortal man.

***

Kia yawned as she slowly stretched, her eyes flickering open to the soft light of her bedroom, made pink by the early morning sunlight shining through the curtains. Turning her head to the side Kia looked at her clock, still half an hour before her alarm was due to go off but she just couldn't sleep any longer. It wasn't every day a girl turned eighteen and Kia intended to enjoy every moment of it.

She could tell by the warmth of her room and the brightness of the sun peaking through her curtains that, at barely eight o'clock, it was already turning into a glorious day. Kia had always loved the fact that she was a summer baby. Not only did it mean that she, almost always, had good weather for her special day but even more importantly when she was younger, Kia never had that terrible experience of sharing her birthday with school. She could think of nothing worse than sitting through double maths when you should be planning a party.

Today's celebrations had been a process of negotiations with Kia's mother finally agreeing that she could spend the evening out with her friends if she would spend the day at home. Considering the night's plans consisted of her first legal drinks at a club in town, the compromise was an easy one to make.

Throwing back her light summer duvet Kia swung her legs out of the bed, her fingers raking through her tousled deep brown hair. She really hoped her locks would behave for the night out, it seemed that no matter how much product or heat she applied to it that perfectly straight style her friends always seemed to achieve always alluded her. There was always a kink here and a flyaway section there, it never seemed to be "just right" and she normally had to settle for "good enough". She decided her hair was a concern for later in the day and tied it back in a hair band and headed for the shower.

Katherine looked up as she heard movement from upstairs, it sounded like her daughter was awake already. While Kia had never been an especially lazy child she had always enjoyed her lie-ins, especially on weekends and holidays, so Katherine was surprised at Kia's early start.

Getting to her feet Katherine wrapped her arms around herself and paced slowly towards the window, absentmindedly chewing on her bottom lip as she watched the early morning breeze making the leaves on the trees in the street dance to a silent melody. It was hard to believe her baby girl was already eighteen years old. The years had flown by so quickly that it seemed only yesterday the midwife had placed that little bundle in Katherine's arms and she had known for the first time in her life that there was someone in the world she would die for, would kill for.

Now that little girl was a woman herself and one day she would hold her own daughter in her arms and feel the unconditional love that was so strong it went beyond words. And she too would one day have to turn her little girl's world upside down just as Katherine was about to do; the knowledge of that pressed down upon her.

Chapter Two

Assaie shivered, her teeth chattering together as she wrapped her arms around herself to try and find some warmth. She had never experienced cold before and, to be frank, she didn't like it very much. Her face felt dry and tight as the bitter wind blew against it and the coarse woollen fabric of her dress scratched at her arms and legs while almost totally failing to provide any adequate protection against the harsh autumn weather.

It had seemed so easy, such a simple choice, to step down from the heavens and embrace a mortal life but as she walked, her feet beginning to ache and form blisters from the rubbing of unfamiliar footwear, Assaie began to question her decision.

What if Aalegth was right? What if she made this sacrifice and he didn't love her? What if she never even found him? The earth looked so different when observed from on high. Now it all seemed a strange dusty brown, with wind that chilled Assaie to the bone, not the intriguing world it had appeared when she was a mere observer.

No. She could not give in to doubts already, her heart was true and her love was strong and, although they could not influence the outcome directly, Assaie knew that her sisters watched over her. They would guide her in the right direction. Somehow she would find him and then she would know the sacrifice was worth it.

As she entered the outskirts of what she hoped was Jacob's village, Assaie took a moment to rest on a low wall. The pain in her feet was almost unbearable, pushing off her sandals Assaie gingerly rubbed at the tender flesh, swollen and red, making her wince at her own touch.

"Are you alright dear?"

Assaie looked up at the sound of a kindly voice. The old woman smiled, adding more wrinkles to an already lined and weather worn face, her smile showed that most of her teeth were missing with the few that remained in varying shades of yellow.

"Do you need any help?"

"Thank you… I… I've travelled a long way and now I…" Assaie stopped, her throat crackled as she spoke, her lips dry and chapped by the wind and she had a sudden overwhelming sense of the distance she had truly journeyed with no idea of where she was even to lay her head that night.

"Here dear," the woman said as she handed Assaie a pouch, pulling out the stopper as she passed it over, "Take a drink of this, you look parched."

Placing the neck of the pouch to her lips Assaie tipped the liquid into her mouth, drinking deeply of the most delicious nectar she had ever tasted, stopping only when her thirst was quenched.

"Thank you," Assaie said handing back the pouch, her eyes shining as she smiled her gratitude. "What was that? It was incredible."

"You must have been thirsty deary, it's only water." The old woman chuckled softly, there was something about the young stranger that made her want to help, to take care of her and see that she came to no harm. "Now where is your cloak? You can't be out in this weather with no cloak. Did you lose it somewhere?"

"I… I never had one… I guess I wasn't very well prepared for my journey."

"So it seems. And where exactly might you be heading?"

"Here. I think. I mean... I'm not sure now... I was looking for someone."

"Ah a man no doubt. Say no more my dear; we have all done foolish things for men. But come. You can't stay here, there's a storm coming and you with not so much as a cloak to keep off the rain. You'll take supper with me, and a bed for the night too. Then maybe tomorrow you will find your young man."

"If you're sure that wouldn't be an imposition?"

"Not at all," The old woman said with another toothless grin. "It would be my pleasure. But tell me, what's your name? People around these parts just call me Mother."

"I'm... my name is..." Assaie hesitated. She couldn't give her true name, no mortal would ever name their child with that of a Goddess, it was unheard of, unacceptable, considered by many to be blasphemy. With no true plan Assaie opened her mouth again, hoping that the sound she made next would pass as a name, "My name is Phae."

"Well now isn't that a pretty name? Come along then Phae. You'd best put those sandals back on if your poor feet can bare it. My house isn't far and supper has been cooking over the fire all day."

Mother moved off at a speed that belied her appearance and Assaie could not help but wonder if the woman was younger than she imagined. Forcing her feet back into the torturous sandals Assaie raced after her saviour, grateful that she would not have to spend the first night as a mortal alone.

Mother's home was simple, a single story stone building separated into rooms by decorated wall hangings that had obviously seen better days. The wooden table and chairs that dominated one of the rooms were battered and well worn, but everything that Assaie could see was scrubbed clean and nothing seemed to be out of place. Mother may not have been a wealthy woman but she took pride in her home and to Assaie, who was more than grateful for the woman's hospitality, the small house felt like a palace.

"There you go dear," Mother said, ladling stew into a pottery bowl and placing it on the table before her guest. "Get that inside you, I bet it's been a while since you had a good hot meal."

"Thank you," Assaie said, taking a tentative taste of the strange looking concoction before her, her teeth sinking easily into the soft piece of potato which almost melted into her mouth, flooding her taste buds with a rich gravy that encouraged her to spoon up more of the stew as quickly as she could manage without burning her lips. "This is good," she mumbled around a mouthful of food, "Very good."

"Just simple fair," Mother said as she took a chair facing her guest and set about her own meal, "But anything tastes good when you're hungry. Now you eat up, there's plenty more if you want it."

Lacing her fingers together Mother bowed her head and closed her eyes. "I give my thanks to the Goddesses for the food on my table," she said quietly, a prayer Assaie had heard countless time but never before had it tugged at her heart in such a way, tears pricked at her eyes as she realised that this woman had probably given such thanks to her and her sisters for many years without ever really knowing that every word of thanks she gave had always reached the hearts of the Goddesses above.

Opening her eyes Mother smiled at Assaie, nodding towards her food. "Come on now, eat up, don't go letting it get cold."

The two women ate in silence until their bowls were clean, mopping up the last of any gravy with chunks of bread. Pushing her bowl away from her Assaie sighed in contentment. Nothing she had ever eaten in the heavens had been as welcome as that simple stew given to her by a stranger. While human hunger was an uncomfortable and unfamiliar sensation, sating it felt truly incredible.

"You're very kind," Assaie said as Mother cleared the table, rinsing the bowls clean and lifting the remaining stew away from the fire, ready to reheat for the next meal. "I don't know how I can repay you... I have no money but if there is anything I can do..."

"Nonsense," Mother replied, raising her hands and shaking her head as she spoke, "It's a poor do if I can't help out a young thing like you, lost and alone on such a bitter night. What would the Goddesses have said if I'd just left you out there to the elements eh? What would my son have said?"

"You have a son?"

"I do," Mother smiled with obvious pride. "I did have two but my William was called to the Goddesses when he was but a babe."

"I'm sorry."

"But my other boy has grown into a strong man, he fills his mother's heart with joy."

"Where is he now?" Assaie asked, her heart had begun racing the moment Mother mentioned a son and she could hardly contain herself with the though that it must be Jacob, why else would it have been Mother who had come to her aid earlier, surely her sisters must have guided the woman in her direction for such a reason.

"He should be home very soon," Mother said, "Truth be told he should be finding himself a wife by now but he just cannot seem to find any woman who captures his heart. Although I would be lying if I was to say I didn't still love having my boy here with me for I will miss him terribly once he does take himself a wife and have a home of his own."

Before Assaie could reply the women heard a noise at the door, the sound of boots stamping off dirt before entering the house. Assaie held her breath as the door opened, seemingly moving inch by painful inch until

Mother's son was revealed standing in the doorway. A tall man, his hands and face rinsed clean from the dirt that still clung to his clothes, his dark hair was messed by the cold winds; his hands flew up to smooth it as he noticed the beautiful stranger that sat at the table.

"Talk of the devil and he shall arrive," Mother said, her mouth in a wide grin as she stood, stepping forward to take her son's hand and usher him into the room. "Come inside now boy and close that door, you're letting the cold air in. And mind your manners for we have company this evening. Say hello to Phae."

The young man smiled, an expression that illuminated his whole face, his deep brown eyes reflecting the smile that begun on his full pink lips.

"A pleasure to meet you Phae," He said, reaching out a hand in greeting, enveloping Assaie's smaller hand completely. "I'm Henry."

Assaie smiled, hoping that the disappointment she felt in her heart wasn't showing on her face. It wasn't Henry's fault that he was not the man she had dreamed would be walking through the door.

"He's a handsome one isn't he?" Mother said with obvious pride.

"Mother please," Henry objected giving her a playful shove before moving to warm himself beside the fire, helping himself to a generous bowl of stew which he ate where he stood.

"He certainly is," Assaie agreed. There was no denying his good looks. His face, although showing some evidence of an outdoor life, was very pleasing to the eye, as were his broad shoulders and very masculine build. But he wasn't Jacob and so Assaie's enthusiasm was somewhat muted.

"This young lady is spending the night with us," Mother informed her son, "So I expect you to be on your best behaviour."

"Am I ever anything else?" Henry said, "If it makes you happier Phae I could easily sleep in the barn tonight."

"There's no need for that," Assaie replied with a shake of her head. "I would not dream of driving your from your home."

"Well at least let me offer you my bed," Henry insisted. "I will be quite comfortable bringing a mattress here by the fire."

"Isn't he a good boy," Mother said, reaching up to ruffle her son's hair affectionately.

All three heads turned at the sound of a knock at the door.

"Oh I had quite forgotten," Henry said, putting his now empty bowl in the sink and moving to the door. "I invited Jac over for supper. Since his mother died I'm sure he rarely has a decent meal, I hope you don't mind another stranger this evening Phae."

"He's a good lad," Mother assured Assaie, "Not as handsome as my Henry but decent all the same."

"Come on in," Henry said as he opened the heavy wooden door. "Grab yourself a bowl... ah yes this is my mother's guest Phae. Phae this is my very good friend Jacob."

Chapter Three

Kia tilted her head as she looked at her reflection in the mirror of her dressing table. Everyone always said she looked just like Katherine and, while Kia could see some similarities she didn't think she had the understated elegant beauty that her mother possessed.

Applying a generous coating of mascara to her lashes Kia sighed wishing, not for the first time, that she had inherited her mother's stunningly long lashes rather than the short stubby ones she seemed to be cursed with. Kia was in no way a vain woman, her daily make up routine consisted merely of mascara and a quick sweep of lip gloss, but she couldn't help but notice the things about herself she would like to change. If only her hair was more controllable, her nose a little straighter, her mouth a little fuller and her waist line a little less full.

Shaking her head Kia laughed at herself, this was no day to be brooding over the thing she wished she was, today was a day to celebrate all that she actually was. Not to mention the fact that it was also the day when she would finally take possession of the car that her mother had spent years saving up to buy for her. They had chosen the black mini together and, despite the fact that it had been purchased almost a whole month ago, Katherine had insisted that her daughter wait until the actual day of her birthday before she could have it.

Katherine had also implied that she had something important to discuss with Kia and she could only assume it was to do with her father. Kia had never met the man who had helped create her; he had left before she was even born. Katherine rarely mentioned him in the last eighteen years and anytime she had, it was apparent to Kia that the memory of the man was painful for her mother. Whoever Kia's father was, he was the man who had clearly broken her mother's heart and that was all Kia needed to know about him. If he suddenly wanted to be a part of her life now after all this time he could forget it. Kia knew where her priorities lay and they were with the woman who bore her, raised her and loved her.

Pulling a soft pink tee shirt over her head Kia took one last look at herself in the mirror. The tee shirt complemented her stone washed jeans perfectly and, although she might never be a beauty, Kia was content enough that she looked okay.

"Happy birthday to me," Kia began to sing at the top of her voice as she skipped down the stairs.

"Is it someone's birthday?" Katherine said, her face lighting up as her daughter entered the room.

"Funny!"

"Isn't ringing any bells... are you sure there's an important birthday today?"

"Only the most important birthday ever," Kia said with conviction.

"Ever? Wow that is quite some birthday then. Who is this lucky birthday girl then?"

"Ha busted! I never said it was a girl!"

"True, you got me there! Happy birthday sweetheart." Kissing her daughter's cheek Katherine pulled Kia into an embrace. She was so grateful that her daughter had never grown into one of those children who felt themselves too old or too cool to still give their mother a hug.

"Thanks mum," Kia said when she was finally released. "So... would there be a little something around here for me by any chance?"

"Something like this?" Katherine asked, pulling a small packet from behind a sofa cushion.

"Oh for me?" Kia said, clapping her hands together with a child like glee before tearing the small parcel open, revealing the expected car key fastened to a key ring in the shape of a pink cat, the letter K fashioned out of small gems on its chest. "Thank you, thank you... shall we go for a drive?"

"Maybe later," Katherine said, "Come and sit here with me for a minute though, I need to talk to you about something."

Sitting on the cream leather sofa Katherine patted the seat cushion next to her, urging her daughter to join her whilst at the same time wishing they could just get in Kia's new car and drive somewhere.

As Kia sat down Katherine looked around the room, a rush of memories flooding her vision. Over by the large bay window that looked out over a small neat garden was where Kia took her first tentative steps, the doorway leading into the kitchen showed marks where each birthday as she grew Kia's height would be recorded, until she grew too old for such things, and here, where they sat now, side by side on the sofa was where the pair would sit, cuddled up under a blanket sharing tissues and chocolates as they watched the latest weepy movie. So many memories and today would mark another one, possibly the most memorable, certainly the most significant.

"I have something else to give you," Katherine said, her fingers twisting around each other as she looked into her daughter's expectant face. It looked so familiar, almost like looking at her own image twenty years earlier when her own mother had passed on what she was about to.

"Mum no, the car is more than enough, you shouldn't have got me anything else."

"I didn't," Katherine said as she removed another package from the sofa, "It's a sort of heirloom I guess... my mother gave it to me on my eighteenth birthday as her mother had given it to her, and now, well now it's to be yours."

"What is it?" Kia asked as she took the plain brown box from her mother and lifted the lid.

Kia froze when she saw what was inside. It wasn't the first time she had seen the pendant that lay on top of tissue paper.

In all of her eighteen years Kia could only remember one time when Katherine had seriously lost her temper. Kia was no more than six years old and indulging in her favourite game of the time, dressing up. Deciding her latest princess outfit needed the right piece of jewellery Kia had gone to raid her mother's jewellery box, discovering to her delight a silver chain from which hung a stylised figure of a woman, arms raise over its head to hold a small purple coloured jewel. It was perfect and Kia had been admiring herself in Katherine's full length mirror when she had been discovered.

Katherine had hit the roof, almost tearing the chain from her daughter's neck as she screamed at Kia to never touch her things again and dragged her into her own bedroom, slamming the door behind her.

Kia had wept hysterically for almost half an hour before Katherine returned to her daughter, pulling the weeping girl onto her knee, rocking her gently as she whispered her apologies into the girl's hair.

Kia had never seen the pendant again, until now.

Taking the pendant from the box Katherine smiled at it for a moment before pressing it into Kia's hand, wrapping the girl's fingers tightly around it; not letting go.

"This is a part of your inheritance Kia," Katherine told her, "A part of who you are... who we are."

"What do you..." Kia stopped speaking as a searing pain tore through the palm of her hand, her eyes widened and tears sparkled against the blue grey of them as she fought to pull her hand from her mother's grip, but Katherine held on tightly, her heart aching for the pain she knew her daughter was feeling, but she knew it was a fleeting and necessary pain.

"Mum please... let go... you're hurting me..."

"I'm sorry sweetheart," Katherine said, tears shimmering in her own eyes at causing Kia such distress. "It won't be for long."

"What are you doing? Stop it... please."

Finally Katherine let go, the pendant dropping to the floor as Kia looked at the mark branded onto her palm.

"Why... what... mum what was that?"

"I'm sorry Kia, I had to..."

"Had to? Look what you've done!"

Kia held out her hand, the mark on her palm glowing red and angry.

"I know," Katherine said, holding out her own hand as an identical mark slowly appeared on her palm. "It will fade in a little while, but it'll always be with you."

"What is it, I don't understand."

"It's what marks us as what we are... it awakens what we will become..."

"What's that supposed to mean?"

"It's the mark of Assaie, the mark of the Goddess."

Chapter Four

Assaie looked down in the small wooden crib in wonder. Despite the fact that her daughter was now almost four months old it still seemed an impossibility that this beautiful little creature was a part of her, of her and Jacob.

From the moment they had met at Mother's, Jacob and Assaie had been inseparable, the attraction between them apparent for all to see and no one had been surprised when they married only a few months after that initial meeting. Their wedding had been a simple but joyous occasion and Assaie had said her own silent prayer when the priestess had asked for the blessings of the Goddesses on their union.

Assaie had never even considered the possibility of a child with her new husband and when she realised she was expecting, an irrational fear had gripped her, she had no idea what being a mother entailed and she didn't know if she would be up to the task. Her fears were quickly quashed and replaced by excitement as soon as she saw Jacob's reaction to the news.

Sweeping his wife up in his arms Jacob had spun Assaie around, laughing as he kissed her and announcing that their child would be the most beautiful and precious ever. He hadn't been wrong.

With Jacob by her side Assaie knew she could achieve anything.

The only thing that would have made Assaie's life better would have been if she could have shared it with her sisters, but she knew they were watching her from above and she knew they would be sharing in her joy.

As was the tradition the naming of a girl child was the sole responsibility of the mother and when Assaie asked Jacob's opinion he smiled and shook his head. "I know you will find the perfect name for our daughter."

For a while Assaie toyed with the idea of naming the child after one of her sisters however she knew the uproar such a name would cause, a stigma that could well follow the child all of her life but she knew so little of human names, how could she choose the right one?

"Jacob?" She began one evening when the baby was already two weeks old and still without a name, "What's Mother's name? All this time and I've never heard anyone call her anything but Mother."

Jacob put the knife he was using down on the table, blowing some loose sawdust from the piece of wood that was slowly becoming a figurine of an animal that was to hang over the child's crib, and he looked at his wife, his brow furrowed as he tilted his head to one side.

"I'm not sure I remember, it's been so long since she was anything but Mother." Running his hands over the wooden model, checking that all possible splinters had been smoothed away Jacob thought hard, memories swirling around his mind until he locked on the one he was searching for. "Of course," he said in triumph, "I remember her telling me once that she was named after a herb that has great healing powers, her name is Althaia."

"A healer," Assaie said, her lips curling into a smile as she thought of it. "Yes, I think our daughter should be called Althaia."

"Of course," Jacob agreed. "It couldn't be anything else."

***

Clearing away the breakfast dishes Assaie whistled quietly to herself. Althaia had polished off her milk and mashed fruit in record time and had even managed to get most of it in her mouth rather than smeared across her face and in her hair. At six months old she was becoming more and more interested in her surroundings with each passing day and each of Jacob's new carvings held his daughter enthralled.

Assaie was surprised at how much pleasure she took in her new life, things as simple as taking care of her home and family were more satisfying than anything she could have imagined. As a Goddess her surroundings were always luxurious and of the utmost comfort. As a human her home was a simple stone building with whitewashed walls, hand woven rugs on the floor and a well worn wooden table with mismatched chairs in the centre of the main living and eating area but to Assaie it was beautiful. She had quickly come to realise that heaven was more than just a location, it was something deep in the heart and with a husband and child who she loved unconditionally she had found heaven again.

The baby stirred in her crib, threatening to cry but not quite committing herself to the effort required to let out the piercing wail that was perfect for shattering her parent's sleep.

"Hush now little one," Assaie said, stroking her fingertips across her child's cheek, "You can't be hungry again so soon, you have an appetite just like your father's."

"Well who would have thought it?"

The unexpected voice in the doorway caused Assaie to spin around quickly, instinctively placing her body between the stranger and her daughter's crib.

"What do you want?" Assaie asked, her gaze taking in the stranger before looking behind her to make sure her daughter was well hidden behind her. "I'm sorry I didn't hear you knock."

The man looked familiar and yet Assaie could not place him, she was certain he was not one of Jacob's friends or anyone she had seen around the village and yet she could not shake the feeling that she knew him from somewhere. His broad shoulders almost filled the narrow doorway, his head only a few inches from its top, making him even taller than Jacob. He was handsome but in an understated way, you might not even notice his looks at first until you took a few seconds to properly look and then his deep dark eyes would appear almost hypnotic. Simply dressed in a tan coloured tunic and trousers he would have blended into the village almost unnoticed but, by the way he stood framed in the doorway with his head held high and feet apart, Assaie got the impression he rather enjoyed being noticed, being the centre of attention.

"No," the man said, "You wouldn't have heard me knock... because I didn't. My, my, my though... just look at you!"

"Who are you? What do you want?"

"Never mind me, what about you? Who exactly are you meant to be?"

"My name is Phae and you're..."

"Come on now, we both know that isn't true... don't we Assaie?"

"I'm sure I don't know what you're talking about." Assaie took an involuntary step backwards, the back of her legs knocking against Althaia's crib, causing the child to begin fussing once more.

"You really don't recognise me? I mean I know down here we look more like them than we do ourselves but still... I knew you the second I saw you walking through the village yesterday."

Assaie looked harder at the man, trying to picture him in different surroundings, away from the life that she knew now. He was familiar, so familiar, if she could just remember.

"Isydro?"

"Ah see, you do remember me, although I go by the name of William down here."

"I, I didn't know that you... that anyone..."

"But just look at you, who would have thought that the great Goddess Assaie would be here playing at wife and mother."

"I'm not playing at anything Isydro, this is my life, the life I chose, that I wanted."

"I always suspected the Goddesses had very limited imagination."

"What are you doing here? What do you want?"

"Relax Assaie, I'm not here to cause you any trouble. I just wanted to thank you actually." As he spoke Isydro strolled casually over to the table in the middle of the room, his fingers mindlessly toying with Jacob's latest carving.

"Thank me? For what?"

"For this," Isydro gestured around himself and towards the still open doorway, "For making it possible for me to come down here and discover just what a human life can offer... I've been wanting to come down here for so long but that damned pact our forebears made had always meant it was impossible for me... at least until one of you decided to take mortal form, then it was open house. I never understood why the elder Gods allowed you Goddesses to have the say in if and when we could walk the earth, but hey, I'm here now... and what a place it can be. I tell you, these human women can be very accommodating if you know what I mean... But then of course you do, I imagine you've indulged yourself in a few "sins of the flesh" since you got down here!"

"I've done no such thing!"

"Come on now... really?"

"I have a husband!" Assaie shook her head, she shouldn't have been surprised by Isydro's comments, of all the Gods he was know to be the most lascivious and his appetite for pleasure knew no bounds.

"Your loss... but if you ever want to..."

"No thank you!"

"Well like I was saying, I was just passing through but I had to stop and say hello once I knew you were here, but don't worry I'm not planning on sticking around, plenty more villages out there for me to enjoy."

"Well don't let me stop you Isydro, and will you please stop playing with that."

"What this?" Isydro held up the carving that he had been turning over in his hands as he spoke.

"Please put it down."

"What is it meant to be?"

"It's a doll... my husband is carving it for our daughter, now please just put it down and leave."

"It's not very good is it?" Isydro said, a laugh mingling with his words as he looked at the figurine with disdain. "Now if I just made a few alterations..." Picking up Jacob's knife Isydro began hacking away at the doll, splinters of wood peeling off and destroying the carving in seconds.

"Isydro stop it," Assaie shouted as she lunged at the former God, grabbing at his hands to pull the figurine from him just as he turned to avoid her grasp.

"I'm just having a moment of fun," Isydro said, throwing out his arms in appeasement as Assaie dove at him once more.

They both knew the moment it happened, the both felt it and they knew what it meant.

With his hands spread wide the ruined carved figurine dropped to the floor, it was already stained with blood, as was Isydro's hand. The knife remained exactly where he had left it, buried deep in Assaie's belly, her blood soaking her dress crimson as the reality of the situation struck her and she felt her legs give way beneath her.

"Help me." Assaie's voice was hardly a whisper, her eyes wide with the shock of what had happened as she waited for the pain that never came. All she could feel was the warmth of her own blood as it pumped from the wound in her belly in time with the beating of her heart.

"I didn't mean... it was an accident." Sinking to his knees at Assaie's side Isydro looked not so much a God but rather a lost little boy faced with the consequences of a prank that had gotten out of hand. "I swear it was an accident."

"I know," Assaie said as she reached for his hand. "Help me, do something... I'm scared."

Gripping Assaie's hand tightly Isydro closed his eyes, his brow creased in concentration as his lips moved in silent invocation.

"Damn it no," Isydro cursed after a moment, throwing Assaie's hand from his grasp with frustration.

As a God, healing such a wound would have taken nothing more than willing it to be gone, but as a mortal, Isydro had no such ability and for the first time he realised just how helpless mortals could truly be.

"I'm sorry, really I am so sorry," Isydro said as he got to his feet, wiping Assaie's blood from his hands, the red stain mingling with the dirt on the front of his tunic, turning it a murky brown. "There is nothing I can do for you..."

"You can't just leave me, please... my daughter..."

"I can't help you... but if I'm found here I will hang, no one would believe this was an accident... I'm sorry... I hope you will be able to forgive me when you return to your sisters..."

"Isydro no, please..." Even as Assaie spoke Isydro had stepped back through the door he had entered, closing it behind him and leaving behind the woman he had fatally wounded.

Closing her eyes Assaie tried to slow her breathing. She could feel her life ebbing away as each beat of her heart caused a little more blood to trickle slowly past the cold metal of the knife's blade. If she could just hold on a little longer, she had to see Jacob one more time, had to tell him before it was too late. She could already feel Death's chilled breath on her neck but she would not give in to him, not yet. Not yet.

Chapter Five

"You're not making any sense," Kia said, absent mindedly rubbing at the mark on her palm, the pain had faded but it still stood out prominently against her pale skin as if burned. "Mum what's going on? What do you mean Goddess?"

"Oh Kia I know this is a lot to take in, a lot to understand, I remember how hard it was when your Grandma gave me the pendant." Katherine smiled gently at her daughter, trying not to feel hurt when Kia flinched from her mother's touch.

"Grandma did this to you?"

"Of course... and her mother to her... it's part of our legacy."

"It's barbaric!" Kia couldn't quite believe that the old woman who had bounced her on her knee as a child had once burned a brand into her daughter's hand, but then a few minutes ago she would have not though her own mother capable of such an act.

"It came from a simpler time," Katherine said with a shrug. Kia had always been such a literal child, it was hardly surprising she should initially question the act rather than the reason. "But it's necessary sweetheart, you will come to understand that before too long."

"I doubt that very much," Kia said, getting to her feet and walking over to the window. This was supposed to be her day, her special day, and now it felt ruined by the one person who she had always been able to count on above all others.

"Give me the chance to explain OK?"

"More about a Goddess?"

"That's right."

"That's nonsense!"

"Is it? I know how you're feeling Kia. It sounds crazy, insane, but a little part of you deep inside can already recognise the truth of what I'm saying. You know in your heart what I'm saying is true."

"But it can't be." Sighing heavily Kia slumped back onto the sofa beside her mother. There was some truth in what Katherine said, despite the impossibility of it all there was something that felt so familiar in her words, they struck at something integral to Kia's being that she had to hear her mother out. "So tell me," she said holding her palm out. "What's this for?"

"I guess you could say it's a trigger... it activates... you... the real you that is."

"Are you saying for the last eighteen years I haven't been the real me?"

"No, no of course not... what I mean is this... the thing it awakens, it completes you... makes you whole."

"Awakens? What do you mean awakens?"

"Your gift."

"Gift... what sort of gift? What do you mean?"

"I don't know," Katherine said, her hands itching to hold her daughter and make everything alright, to make it all make sense, but she knew that would take time. Time and understanding. "It's different for each of us."

"So how do I know what it is?"

"You'll find it... or it'll find you... but it's there now, ready for you."

"And you... you have this gift thing?"

"Yes."

"And Grandma?"

"Well... yes..."

"You didn't sound sure about that."

"It's complicated... Grandma... what she got... it was too much for her ..."

"Too much... why?" Kia rubbed her temples as the beginnings of a headache began to creep into her brain. This was not how she expected the morning to turn out. By now she should have been driving her mother somewhere in her new car, maybe up to the lake for a picnic or to a quiet bar for a pub lunch. Not sitting hearing stories about a Goddess and special gifts. She desperately wanted to get back into bed and let the day start over again.

"I really have to tell you all of this from the very start Kia, otherwise you'll just keep having more questions. So how about you let me tell you exactly what Grandma told me and her mother told her okay?"

"I guess so."

"So it all happened like this... a very long time ago the Goddess Assaie fell in love with a mortal man and she couldn't bear to go on without being with him..."

***

The darkness was almost complete, through the fog Assaie could hear Althaia crying. She didn't know if her daughter needed food or changing or just the comfort of her mother but Assaie could no longer offer any of those things, she would never again get to hold her child, to be with her husband. Assaie's mortal life was coming to an end and she would have to watch her family carry on without her from the heavens but, despite her life being cut short, Assaie wasn't sorry she had taken the chance. She had found the love she sought and she knew that a part of her would always walk the earth, that the love she had shared with Jacob and born a line of daughter's that she would watch over for as long as they needed her.

Whistling as he opened the door Jacob dropped the sack of carrots he had been bringing home the moment he saw his wife's collapsed form lying in a pool of blood. Her face was deathly pale and her eyes closed, the sight was enough to cause Jacob's heart to stop and he gasped for breath at the physical pain the sight gave him. Despite the growing cries of Althaia Jacob could not spare a moment to check on his daughter but rather raced straight to his wife's side, throwing himself down on the floor beside her.

"Phae... oh my Goddess Phae, talk to me please..."

"Jacob?" Assaie's eyes flickered open slowly, the corners of her mouth turning up at the corners slightly. "I knew you would get to me in time ... I couldn't bear to leave you without saying goodbye..."

"Nonsense," Jacob said, tears welling in his eyes as he realised just how much blood was pooled around his wife. "You're not going anywhere my love... I won't allow it."

"I don't think you can stop it dear heart... I so wanted to grow old with you... there were so many things still to experience... you'll have to do them for me now Jacob."

"Phae no, you can't leave us... how can I raise our daughter alone? How can I live without you at my side?"

"You can and you will," Although weak Assaie's voice was determined and with her last ounce of strength she grabbed her husband's hand. "I have to tell you Jacob, I need you to know who I really am."

"You're my beautiful wife Phae, I know exactly who you are..."

"I'm sorry Jacob but I lied to you." Assaie's hand fell away as the last of her strength left her and her final words came out as barely a whisper before she slipped into eternal sleep in the arms of the man she loved. "My name is Assaie."

Burying his face into his wife's dress Jacob wept, his body shook with gasping sobs as his heart broke. From her crib Althaia wailed, her cries blending with those of her father and they shared in a pitiful lament. Jacob had no idea what Phae had meant by her final words but none of that mattered now, all that he could think of was the fact that she was gone and he didn't know how he was supposed to go on without her.

"Don't cry for me Jacob."

The sudden voice started Jacob, causing him to jump to his feet as he roughly scrubbed the tears from his face.

"Who are..." Jacob's words died on his lips, his eyes widening in disbelief as he saw what was not possible. Turning his head to look back at Phae, Jacob confirmed that his wife was still lying motionless on the scrubbed stone floor, So how was she also now standing before him?

Yet this wasn't Phae. She looked the same and yet different. Physically identical, the only obvious difference being the brilliant white gown she now wore, a garment which almost seemed to glow. She almost seemed to glow. There was only one answer.

"Are you a ghost?"

"My sweet gentle Jacob… did I not tell you who I was just a moment ago?"

"I don't understand."

"I think you do." Assaie stepped forward, taking Jacob's hand in her own as she smiled sadly. She so badly wanted to stay but she knew she had the briefest of moments before she would be recalled to the heavens. "My name is Assaie."

"Like the Goddess."

"Exactly."

"Are you?"

"I am."

"How? Why?"

"I wish I had long enough to explain my darling, but just know that I came to earth, became a mortal, because I love you… for the rest of your days know that… I will always watch over you now, both of you."

"Assaie?" Jacob said the name in wonder. This was one of the three Goddesses to whom he prayed, so how could she be standing before him, how could she be telling him she was his wife? "It's not possible."

"But it is, because I am here…"

"I can't believe this is real… my wife… she just… you just… what happened?"

"It was just an accident Jacob, I don't want you to waste your time blaming anyone or seeking revenge… Isydro didn't mean to…" Assaie stopped short, realising she had revealed more than she intended.

"Isydro… the God? He's here… he did this to Phae… to you?"

"Like I said, it was an accident. Jacob please don't go blaming the Gods for this mistake, I don't want our daughter raised with hatred in her heart; can you promise me that?"

"But…" Jacob stopped, one look from Assaie and he could not refuse her, not as a Goddess or a mortal woman.

"I need you to do something else for me Jacob." Unfastening a pendant that hung around her neck, a simple silver chain from which hung a stylised figure of a woman with arms raise over its head to hold a small purple coloured jewel, Assaie pressed it into Jacob's hand. "When our daughter comes of age I need you to give her this, tell her who I was and let her know that I am always with her. Do this for me Jacob and tell Althaia to pass it to her daughter… let our daughters pass this down through the generations and I will always be with them."

"I will. I promise."

"I have to go now."

"No stay a little longer, please…"

"I can't, my time on earth has come to an end. Farewell my love… I love you."

Jacob reached out his hands to grab onto Assaie's arm, to hold onto her for one more moment, but it was already too late. The Goddess had gone.

"Phae… Assaie… wait…"

***

Kia wiped away a tear from her cheek. "Poor Jacob," she said with a sniffle as her mother finished talking. "But he kept his promise?"

"Of course." Katherine looked down at the pendant that still lay on the floor where Kia had dropped it. "You can pick it up now, it won't burn again."

Tentatively Kia picked up the necklace, her eyes wide with wonder as she tried to rationalise this simple pendant as once hanging around the neck of a Goddess. "So this?"

"It was the Goddess Assaie's. By giving it to Jacob she knew she was leaving us a tremendous gift."

"You said gifts before, but I don't understand what you mean. What gifts? Are we like superheroes? Can I fly or something?"

Katherine couldn't hold back her laugh and the sound broke the tension that had been growing between mother and daughter. "Of course not," Katherine said before pausing to think. "At least I don't think so... I've certainly never heard of that ever happening."

"So what then? What did you get?"

Running her thumb over the palm of her hand Katherine smiled. "I was given the gift of empathy."

"Isn't that something people have anyway?"

"To some degree yes, but what I can feel is... more... did you never notice how you could never get away with lying to me?"

"I just thought that was because you were my mum."

"Even the best mother can't spot every lie their child tells, but I can... what you feel I can feel, whatever it is... I know when someone is hurt or upset.... or lying... or cheating." A look of sadness clouded Katherine's face and she turned away from her daughter just as Kia made the connection.

"Like my father?"

Katherine nodded. "At first I tried to ignore it, but I could feel his guilt, each time he touched me it was like a knife in my heart... oh I'm sorry Kia you don't need to hear this..."

"That's all right," Kia said, squeezing her mother's hand, smiling as she knew he mother could feel the love and understanding she couldn't always put into words.

"But what about Grandma?" Kia asked after a few minutes of silence. "You said something about her gift being too much?"

"It was always said that the Goddess never gave us a gift we could not cope with, but sometimes we just don't feel up to the challenge. Grandma could not meet the challenge of her gift."

"What was it?"

"She got sight."

"Sight?"

"Grandma was given the ability to see the future."

"Wow! She should have tried to see the winning lottery numbers one week!"

Katherine shook her head with a smile, trust that to be Kia's first thought. "Unfortunately it didn't quite work like that. Grandma couldn't pick and choose what she saw... she just got visions sometimes..."

"Bad ones?"

"Some were."

"What like?"

"Terrible accidents... one time she saw a car crash just a few miles from her house and she managed to get there and prevent it... she saved people from dying that day."

"But that's amazing... isn't it?"

"It is... and she thought she had been given the most wonderful gift in the world... And then she saw a plane crash... it wasn't even in this country, she tried calling the police but who is going to believe an eighteen year old girl who claims to have visions of a plane going down?"

"What happened?"

"It crashed, and Grandma was haunted by dreams of the visions she had had, she knew that the screams and the deaths she saw were all real... she couldn't cope."

"What did she do?" Kia couldn't quite picture her grandmother as an eighteen year old, never mind having to live with such awful visions.

"There is one last part to the gift from Assaie," Katherine said. "Something we all have to decide after twelve months."

"What's that?"

"To keep your gift... or to reject it forever..."

"How? What do you do... what does it mean?"

"On your nineteenth birthday, if whatever gift the Goddess has given you isn't something you feel you can handle you just hold onto the pendant, like earlier, and ask her to take it away from you."

"And then?"

"It's gone... but it's a one-time thing, if you reject it then it's gone forever, there is no changing your mind. Grandma often wondered if she couldn't have ended up doing a lot of good with her visions if she'd only been a little stronger."

Kia was silent for a while as she looked at the pendant in her hand. It was a lot to take in, it didn't seem possible and yet she knew it was.

"I wonder what my gift will be?"

Chapter Six

Katherine and Kia sat quietly for some time, each in silent reflection of the morning's events. For one it was the culmination of eighteen years waiting, for the other it was an unexpected revelation that would take some getting used to.

"What about that drive?" Katherine said after some time. "It is still your birthday and that car isn't going to drive itself."

"I don't know… I'm not sure I feel much like celebrating any more… maybe I should call the girls and cancel tonight too."

"You will not." Katherine's voice was so stern that Kia looked at her in surprise, if anything she had expected her mother to approve of the idea. "Kia Deering you only turn eighteen once in your life and you have to enjoy it. I know that everything I have told you will take some getting used to but that does not mean you have to stop living in the meantime. Now come on, show me what a sensible driver you can be and that it wasn't a mistake getting you that car!"

The rest of the day turned into more of the type of day Kia had anticipated. After a few minutes trying to coax her hair into something that at least resembled a style Kia had given up and tied it back once more before slipping on her trainers and grabbing her new car key. There was no denying that despite everything else, she was still excited to be able to finally drive her very own car. She had passed her test almost four months earlier, spurred on by the promise that if she passed she would get a car for her birthday. Kia knew that her mother had worked extra hours and saved every penny she could to buy the car and in Kia's eyes it was the most amazing vehicle she had ever seen. The black paintwork gleamed in the August sun and as she opened the driver's door Kia caught the scent of vanilla from a discreet cat shaped air freshener hanging from the rear view mirror. Katherine had added as many personal touches as she could afford to and the site of the bright pink seat covers made Kia smile. Everything about the car was just how she would have chosen herself. It was perfect.

"So where are we going?" Kia asked as her mother slipped into the passenger seat and clicked her seatbelt into place.

"You're the driver," Katherine said with a smile as she settled back into her seat and looked dead ahead. "You tell me where we're going."

The lakeside pub was over an hours' drive, the last twenty minutes including some quiet picturesque roads with quaint cottages that seemed to have remained unchanged over the centuries. The drive had been a joy for both driver and passenger. The former pleased she could prove to her mother that she was a sensible driver, the latter relieved to see that her daughter really did know what she was doing behind the wheel of a car.

"Mum," Kia said as she looked out over the water, sipping at the glass of pineapple juice she had ordered from the bar, as much as she would have liked to join her mother in the small glass of wine she was nowhere near a confident enough driver to risk even the smallest amount of alcohol in her system.

"Yes sweetheart."

"Do you think if I got sight I would be able to cope with it?"

Katherine considered the question for a while before answering. "I think you can cope with whatever the Goddess chooses for you."

"Thanks… and mum?"

"Yes?"

"Thanks for the car, it really is awesome."

"You're welcome sweetheart, you deserve it. And you will be sensible in it won't you? Even when you're with your friends."

"I promise."

Katherine smiled and nodded. Even without her gift of empathy she knew that her daughter meant what she said. She was lucky to have raised such a sensible girl and Katherine couldn't have been more proud. Whatever gift Kia received she knew her daughter was more than capable of rising to the challenge.

***

Applying a final coat of baby pink lip gloss Kia checked herself over in the mirror. Her new black dress was just perfect, tight enough to emphasise a few curves but not too tight as to cling to the parts she would rather hide. Her hair was shining and almost straight. While not vain enough to ever think she could pass for beautiful, Kia was content enough with how she looked. She toyed with the thought of finishing off her outfit with the Goddess pendant but the thought of possibly losing it made her change her mind and instead opted for the small silver K with a diamond sparkling at the bottom of the initial.

Entering the living room Kia span around for her mother's approval.

"Will I do?"

"You look beautiful," Katherine said with sincerity. While she knew that her daughter often doubted herself, in so many ways, Katherine could always see the girl's beauty, both inside and out. "You have a wonderful time... but don't go over doing it okay?"

"I won't."

"I know it's your birthday but..."

"I won't be stupid mum," Kia promised, "I have no intention of spending the day tomorrow in bed with a hangover! There's little enough of the summer break left before college starts again, I plan on enjoying it."

Katherine nodded her approval. She could always count on her sensible, clever, beautiful daughter. Her daughter's friends on the other hand were not always so reliable, and when the three of them got together they did tend to egg each other on. Kia still had the scar on her right thigh from the time Rebekah had dared her to climb that tree, although to be fair they were only seven years old at the time.

"I'd better get going, Rebby will be wondering where I am."

"You're not walking are you? I know it's still light out but..."

"Don't worry mum, I'm just walking round the corner to Rebby's then we're gonna get a taxi into town. Sofia's dad is dropping her off at the club so we're meeting her outside."

"Have a wonderful time darling."

"Thanks mum," Kia said, kissing her mother briefly on the cheek, leaving a small pink lip gloss stain. "Mum?"

"Yes?"

"Would you be cross if I told the girls... you know... about the Goddess stuff?"

Katherine smiled slightly, she remembered that same thought twenty years earlier when she had such an amazing secret to tell. "It's up to you sweetheart, it's a part of you and it's your choice who you share it with."

Yeah," Kia said thoughtfully, running her fingers through her hair as she looked in the mirror, her head slightly tilted on one side in contemplation. "Yeah... maybe not yet though... I'll think about it."

Her mind made up Kia grabbed her small red bag. "Night mum," she called back over her shoulder as she headed out of the front door. "Don't wait up!"

Rebekah was already waiting at her front door when Kia arrived. Slightly taller and far more slender than her, Rebekah had the willowy grace that Kia envied. Combined with almost perfect auburn hair, blemish free skin and stunning sea green eyes she was the kind of girl Kia could have been seriously jealous of, if she didn't love her that was.

"Finally!" Rebekah said throwing her arms up in the air, "I thought you were never coming!"

"I'm five minutes late!"

"That's five minutes of drinking time birthday girl!"

"I've already told you I'm not getting wasted tonight," Kia said, hugging her friend in their familiar greeting.

"Whatever!" Rebekah said with a grin. "Happy birthday anyway."

"Thank you," Kia said, her eyebrows slightly arched expectantly. "And?"

"And what?"

"You know we can't call a taxi till you've given me my present."

"What makes you so sure I got you anything?"

"Rebby!" Kia said in fake shock. Since they had been old enough to have money of their own the three friends had never failed to buy each other birthday and Christmas presents.

"Here then," Rebekah said holding out an unwrapped chocolate bar, a long standing joke between the two of them. At nine years old Rebekah had bought a small chocolate bar for her friend with her minimal pocket money, despite the fact that Kia had never actually liked chocolate. Two weeks later Kia had given the very same bar back in celebration of Rebekah's birthday.

"You know I think you should just keep that," Kia said with a grin, "Save me bothering to give it back to you!"

"Such ingratitude," Rebekah said wiping away invisible tears. "I don't suppose you want this either?"

Kia grabbed the small parcel wrapped in shiny pink paper straight out of her friend's hand.

"Oh what is it?" She said, shaking the box and turning it over. Kia had always found half the fun in presents is the moment of wonder before actually unwrapping it.

"It's nothing much," Rebekah said, stepping a little uncertainly from one foot to the other. She never felt her gifts lived up to those of her friends. No matter how hard she tried or how much she saved, she always felt that the presents her friends picked were far superior.

"I already love it 'cause it's from you," Kia insisted.

"Soppy," Rebekah teased, secretly grateful for the sentiment.

Unable to wait any longer Kia tore at the paper, quickly reducing it to shreds around her feet as she revealed the black box inside which she opened without a moment's hesitation.

"I love it!" Kia said with genuine glee as she lifted the small silver bangle from its box and slipped it around her wrist. It was a perfect fit and complimented her outfit exactly.

"Really?"

"Really! It's gorgeous, thank you."

Standing in the hallway while Rebekah telephoned for a taxi, Kia admired her new bangle, turning it this way and that to admire how the light caught on the small lines engraved into it, beautifully illustrating the daisies that were carved into the silver.

The two girls giggled and chatted during the short car journey to the club, almost tumbling out of the taxi in their excitement for what the night might hold for them.

Spotting a blue car across the road Kia raised her hand in greeting and seconds later Sofia stepped from the vehicle, stopping for a moment to lean back into the car and say goodnight to her father before she half ran, half skipped across the road to embrace her friends.

The smallest of the three friends, Sofia carried a little extra weight which was made more noticeable by her lack of height, but the brightness of her smile and warmth of her soft brown eyes made the word "pretty" be the first one that came to mind when people met her.

Kia's gift was already in Sofia's hand as she reached the birthday girl, ready to press it into her friend's eager grasp.

More pink wrapping paper was quickly discarded and another gift revealed to Kia's excitement and joy.

"You two planned this," Kia said, pulling matching earrings from the box.

"Do you like them?" Sofia asked, smiling as Kia took out the plain hoops she had been wearing and replaced them with the small daisies, the fading light catching on the small jewels that formed the centre of the flower making them sparkle.

"They're gorgeous, thank you... thank you both."

"Now come on ladies," Rebekah said, looping her arms with her two best friends. "The night awaits us."

Chapter Seven

The music vibrated though Kia's body as she danced, swaying in time to the music, though not as much as Rebekah. Having taken the need to party as literally as she could manage Rebekah had raised countless shots in celebration of Kia's birthday, downing her own and those of her friends when the other girls decided they had had enough. Kia didn't envy the hangover Rebekah was going to be facing the next day.

Laughing loudly Rebekah threw her arms in the air and spun around causing her to lose her balance. Kia and Sofia reached out to catch her arms but she slipped through their fingers, stumbling backwards into the crowd.

Kia gasped as her friend began to fall, heading towards the ground at a rapid speed, prevented from crashing to the ground with some force at the last second by the sudden intervention of a pair of arms that caught her and, with some effort, managed to get her back to her feet.

"Rebby are you okay?" Kia asked, taking her friends hands and squeezing them tightly.

"I just tripped," Rebekah said, her words slurred as she wavered slightly, Kia's hold on her hands the only thing keeping her from slipping to the ground again.

"Come on," Kia said as she started to lead Rebekah and Sofia from the dance floor. "Let's go and have a sit down for a bit."

"Oh if you want to," Rebekah agreed, stumbling along. "You are the birthday girl after all, so whatever you wants we does... do... oh you know..."

"I'll get her some water," Sofia said once Rebekah had been settled safely on one of the clubs overstuffed red sofas that lined the far wall, just far enough from the main music and dance floor that they could actually hear each other without having to resort to hand gestures.

"She all right?"

Kia turned at the sound of the male voice behind her, she hadn't noticed the man following them from the dance floor as she had been more concerned about getting her friend seated safely.

"Just one too many," Kia said, unable to stop herself from smiling back at the man whose own smile seemed disarmingly contagious. "Could have been worse if you hadn't caught her, lucky you were there."

"Not really," he said, "I was kind of watching."

Kia could have sworn his cheeks flushed pinkly for a moment, but it could have been a reflection of the lights flashing in the club.

"Oh well, you can't really miss Rebby can you?" Kia said, hoping her smile remained gracious and didn't reflect the sudden hit of disappointment she felt. There was no denying the man was attractive, tall and slender but not thin, there was a definite hint of muscle beneath his carefully ironed striped shirt, his smile showed a deep dimple in his right cheek and his eyes, that were either blue or grey, sparkled as he smiled. Of course he was going to notice Rebekah though, she was hard to miss when she was sober never mind drunk, and even when she had had a few too many she still had the ability to turn many a head.

"I suppose not," the man said, the pink colour flashing across his cheeks again as he ran a hand through his hair, causing it to stick up here and there which, rather than detract from his good looks, seemed to enhance them. "But it wasn't actually her I was watching."

"Oh?"

"She just happened to be standing between us when she fell."

"Oh... oh right... you mean it was...?"

"Yeah... your other friend."

"Yeah, right... of course." Kia turned towards the bar where Sofia was desperately trying to get served a glass of water but her short stature meant she had been over looked several times already. "She should be back in a minute." Her eyes burning into the back of Sofia's head Kia wished her friend would hurry up back to save her from the excruciating embarrassment she felt as her own cheeks glowed bright red, and she couldn't even pretend the colour was from the disco lights.

"Sorry... that was meant to be a joke... not a very good one... can I start again?"

"Not sure I follow you."

"Hi," the man said offering his hand to Kia. "My name's Xander. I noticed you earlier and wondered if I could buy you a drink or something."

"It is her birthday," Rebekah's drunken voice shouted from the sofa.

"In that case happy birthday," Xander said, realising he still had his hand outstretched hand and awkwardly stuffed it into his jeans pocket. "So. A drink?"

"I don't know," Kia said. "I think I probably need to get my friend home."

"Right of course. Look I'm sorry about the stupid joke... my mates always tell me I'm not very funny."

"No it's fine, really…"

"I think I'm gonna throw up," Rebekah said as she struggled to her feet, swaying worse than ever, her head turning this way and that as she tried to locate the ladies room.

"Come on Rebs," Sofia said, appearing as if from nowhere and putting a pint glass of water on the table in front of the sofa before putting her arm around her friend's waist and guiding her away. "You stay here and chat K," Sofia said with a grin and a nod towards Xander who was standing awkwardly to one side. "Me and Rebby will be fine."

Kia and Xander stood for a moment in silence, shuffling their feet slightly and casting glances at each other before quickly looking away.

"So," Xander said finally. "That drink?"

"Why not," Kia said, "But just a coke."

"No problem, why don't you sit down and I'll nip to the bar."

Settling onto the sofa that her friend had just vacated Kia watched Xander as he made his way to the bar. He ran his hands through his hair once more as he walked, smoothing the tufts that he had dislodged earlier. Kia couldn't deny the flurry of butterflies that seemed to have taken up residence in her stomach over the last few minutes, although she thought she was being quite foolish it wasn't an entirely unpleasant experience and she couldn't tame the wide smile as Xander returned with two glasses. Both appeared to be coke but one had a small paper umbrella in it and a ring of pineapple on the rim, the embellished drink he handed to Kia.

"I did just want a coke," Kia said sniffing at the glass to see if there was any alcohol in it.

"I know, and it is… but as it's your birthday I asked them to jazz it up a bit. Cheers."

Kia clinked her drink against Xander's as he settled onto the sofa next to her, the overstuffed cushions causing him to roll a little closer to her than he might have purposefully decided to sit but neither of them felt the need to move or object.

"So anyway," Xander said after taking a sip of his drink and placing it on the table, "You know my name but you've not told me yours."

"You're right I haven't," Kia said, deliberately taking a long drink of her coke before saying anything further. "It's Kia."

"That's quite an unusual name," Xander said, one eyebrow arched, another thing about him that Kia found disarmingly attractive.

"Says the man called Xander," Kia replied, placing her own glass on the table, subconsciously setting it down close to Xander's.

"Well it's Alexander really... but that just sounds too... I dunno... poncey?"

"Whereas Xander sounds what?"

"Cool of course."

"But of course. Never fancied just being an Alex?"

"Why be just something when you can be exceptional?" Xander said, emphasising the X in the word exceptional.

"Oh I see, is that what you are?"

"Well you'll just have to find out for yourself I suppose."

Kia flushed slightly and reached for her drink to give her something to do as she composed herself. Xander really was sitting very close, she was sure he had got closer since they started talking even though she wasn't aware of him moving. She could feel the heat from his leg pressing against her own, painfully aware that only two strips of fabric kept their bare flesh separate.

"How am I supposed to do that?" Kia asked, suddenly feeling disappointed as she saw her friends returning from the ladies. Rebekah looked pale and shaky, her hair was damp where Sofia had obviously been washing her face.

"Sorry," Sofia mouthed as they approached.

"Looks like it's time for me to be going," Kia said, getting to her feet and smoothing her dress down. "Thanks for the drink."

"It was nice to meet you all," Xander said, including all three girls in his statement but his eyes fixed entirely on Kia.

"We'll see you outside," Sofia said to Kia, once again leading Rebekah away, "I think this one needs some air."

"See you in a second," Kia said, reluctant to leave but, no matter how nice Xander seemed she wasn't stupid enough to remain in a club with a strange man. "I really should be going," Kia said once her friends had gone.

"Of course… it was nice to meet you though… maybe I could have your number?" Xander grinned hopefully, giving him the look of a small boy which made it impossible not to smile at him.

"I'm not sure," Kia said. Kia was very sure that she wanted to give Xander her number but she had only just met him and he could be anyone, the sensible side of her argued against doing the thing her heart urged her to.

"Okay," Xander said, disappointment clear in his voice. "How about I give you my number? Then if you want to call or text you can… and if you don't… well… I hope you do."

Xander watched for a few minutes as Kia caught up with her friends by the exit and the three of them turned to leave the club. Weaving slowly between the other patrons, the drunken girl was clearly being both held upright and propelled along by her companions.

Finally, once they were out of sight, Xander wandered slowly back to his own friends without the swagger that normally accompanied his return from chatting up his latest potential conquest.

"Well?" Jason's grin was wide as he tilted his head questioningly to the side, one eyebrow rose giving him a comical look that Xander could not help but laugh at.

"Well what?" Xander said, knowing all too well the larger question behind the word but for once unsure just how much of his encounter with the intoxicating Kia he really wanted to share.

"Don't tell me the studmeister finally struck out!" Jason's eyes widened in feigned shock as he nudged his friend playfully.

Being a good few inches shorter than his friend and with looks that were not as instantly alluring, Jason could have easily ended up resenting Xander's frequent successes with the opposite sex, but his nature was such that Jason took each of his own successes and failures with equal good humour. However, that did not mean that he wasn't more than happy to tease his friend any time that Xander's tried and tested lines failed to hit their target, and as that was a rare event, Jason seized the opportunity with glee.

"I don't see the ladies flocking around you right now," Xander said with a flourish of his arms as if to emphasise the space around them which was devoid of female presence.

"I wasn't the one trying to pull." Jason chuckled as he dragged his fingers through his scruffy dark blonde hair. No matter how hard he had tried to style it Jason's hair had proved uncontrollable and eventually he decided it was easier just to let it do its own thing and somehow, one he had stopped battling with it, it had settled into a disorganised arrangement that seemed to suit him perfectly.

"Ah come on now Jase," Marty chipped in once he had drained his bottle of lager and placed the empty on the bar. "It can't be easy for Xand to discover he's losing his touch... go easy on him eh?"

The taller of the three friends Marty had always been the least successful when it came to the opposite sex but that fact never seemed to phase him and he happily played the role of 'wing man' without question or complaint on countless occasions.

"You two are just hilarious, d'you know that?" Xander said with a roll of his eyes, reaching for the bottle of lager he had left on the bar when he'd gone over to talk to Kia. "And who drank my beer?"

Marty smiled and raised his shoulders in a half shrug. "What? We didn't expect you to be coming back... how was I to know you'd be getting the knock back?"

"I did not get the knock back."

"Well she left without you," Jason teased, turning his head back towards the bar he raised one hand to get the barman's attention and ordered three more bottles.

"Her mate was wasted..."

"Right," Marty nodded, "So you got her number then?"

"Err... not exactly..."

"Come on Xand," Jason said, pushing a cold beer into his friend's hand. "This is like pulling teeth mate... you're not normally so cagey about the birds you pull..."

Xander took a slow deep drink of his beer, both to quench his thirst but also to delay his need for response.

It was true that Xander had had many a success with the ladies. He had an ability to charm in a way that reduced them to putty in his hands and that was a situation he was often more than happy to exploit for his own pleasure without always considering the feelings of the girl whose emotions he would be toying with. As he matured Xander's attitude mellowed and he sought something a little more meaningful in his encounters, but he still enjoyed female company and was rarely short of offers.

Xander felt an unexpected pang of guilt and he struggled to swallow his beer. He had no idea how many times he had promised to call a girl only to delete her number before she had even got out of sight and never give her a second thought. It would serve him right if Kia was, at that very moment, deleting his number from where he had eagerly keyed it into her mobile. Yet he seriously hoped that she wasn't.

"Nah," Xander said after a considerable pause. "I wasn't trying to pull her..."

"So what were you trying then?" Marty asked.

"I was... I dunno... just getting to know her."

Jason opened his mouth to tease Xander some more but he stopped as he saw something that almost seemed to shimmer in his friends deep blue grey eyes. Jason couldn't quite put a name to it but whatever it was he knew that something inside Xander had changed in that short meeting with the girl in the club, and changed for the better.

Outside the club Rebekah was sniffling loudly, fresh tears springing from her eyes as Kia approached.

"I am so sorry," she said, wiping tears and mascara across her cheeks. "I've ruined your birthday haven't I?"

"No of course you haven't," Kia said, her smile genuine as she gave Rebekah a soft squeeze. "I've had the most amazing night."

"Promise?"

"I promise."

"Did you give him your number," Sofia asked as the three began to walk slowly in the direction of the taxi rank, joining the back of a long queue despite it not even being 1am yet.

"No I didn't."

"K! Why ever not?" Sofia said, her eyes wide with disbelief. "He was gorgeous."

"I know," Kia replied, her smile illuminating her whole face. "That's why I took his!"

Taking her mobile phone out of her handbag Kia tapped a brief message onto the screen before keying in a number and hitting send.

"I decided to text," the message read. "Call me some time. Kia."

Back inside the club Xander's pocket began to vibrate, fishing out his mobile he could have jumped for joy as he read the message. Quickly saving Kia's number to his phone's memory Xander didn't notice the grins of his friends as his fingers flew over the keys before he held the phone to his ear.

"Hey," Xander said as the call was quickly answered. "Is now too soon to call?"

Chapter Eight

Kia and Sofia chatted in the back of the taxi while Rebekah dozed at Sofia's side. Kia could hardly contain her excitement at the date she had arranged with Xander for the following night and the girls were mentally going through the contents of Kia's wardrobe in search of the perfect outfit.

"It has to be kinda sexy... but not slutty," Sofia advised, turning her head every now and again to check that Rebekah was still all right.

"Excuse me," Kia said in mock offence. "I don't own anything slutty I will have you know!"

"What about that pale blue dress?"

Kia pictured the item her friend referred too, it was true it was hardly a garment that contained a lot of fabric, and had barely covered her underwear the one time she had been brave enough to wear it.

"That doesn't count," Kia said, "It was just an impulse buy... there's no way I would wear that on a first date... or ever again come to think of it."

"So what are you going to wear?"

"I really don't know." Kia furrowed her brow, chewing at her bottom lip as she tried to think of something. The one item of clothing that would have been perfect was the dress she was currently wearing. "Maybe I could get something new." She said at last with a grin, already planning a shopping trip in her head and for the first time she would be able to drive her and her friends somewhere. "You reckon Rebs will be up for it in the morning?"

Looking at their friend Sofia laughed and shook her head. "I don't think she's going to be up for anything other than sleeping and feeling very sorry for herself."

"I guess… but she always knows what looks right…"

"We can always text her photos?"

"We can! Brilliant idea!"

Closing her eyes for a second Kia couldn't hold back the smile as the image of Xander popped into her mind, his hair slightly out of place as he ran his hands nervously through it. There was something so very appealing about him and, although they hadn't had very long to talk, she already hoped he was going to be a fixture in her life for a long time to come.

The first indication the girls had of any problem was the sudden blaring of a car horn that caused Rebekah to jump, startled awake. The horn was followed by a painful screeching of breaks before the car came to an abrupt violent stop. The three girls gasped as their seat belts cut into shoulders and stomachs, the sudden halting of the vehicle wrenching their bodies uncomfortably.

"Is everyone alright?" Kia asked when she could finally find her breath again.

"Sof?"

"Yeah, yeah I think so."

"Rebby?"

"What happened?" Rebekah suddenly felt acutely sober and her head throbbed so badly it felt ready to explode.

"I don't know I..." Kia stopped abruptly as she looked towards the front of the vehicle. The front windscreen was shattered, a spattering of blood on the broken shards of glass where the driver had been thrown through. "Call an ambulance," she said feeling suddenly and surprisingly calm as she unfastened her seatbelt and opened the car door.

"Oh shit, oh shit," Sofia said, her gaze fixed on the bloody windscreen and her hands trembling as she tried not to imagine what lay beyond.

"Where... what..." Rebekah's voice grew high pitched and hysterical as she registered what had happened to the driver. "Oh god, oh god, oh god... is he dead? What if he's dead..."

"Sof phone an ambulance... now!" Kia shouted.

While Sofia fumbled in her bag for her mobile phone Kia raced around to the front of the car. From the back seat she hadn't been able to see the other vehicle which it appeared they had hit side on, crushing both the driver's door and the front of the taxi. The driver, and sole occupant, of the other vehicle was motionless, blood covering his face as it ran freely from a large cut in his forehead.

"Are you all right?" She shouted, the driver's eyes flickering open in acknowledgement. "It's okay, we've called an ambulance... just stay where you are."

Racing around to the driver's side of the taxi Kia stopped dead, the taxi driver was sprawled across the road before the car, his leg at a painfully unnatural angle, his body bloodied from the many cuts he sustained from the windscreen's glass. The thing that made Kia stop and take a deep breath however were his eyes, wide open and staring up at the sky unblinking, they showed no sign of life.

Approaching him slowly Kia took some deep steadying breaths, she had taken a few first aid courses in college but nothing could have prepared her for this.

"Hello?" She said as she crouched down beside him. "Hello can you hear me?"

Getting no reaction Kia reached out a hand and gently shook the taxi driver's shoulder.

"Hello?" She said again, already knowing that it was too late for him to ever hear her again but unable to stop trying. "Please be all right... hello?"

Kneeling down closer to the driver Kia leaned over, holding her hair back, as she tried to listen for any sounds of breath but there were none, his eyes still stared lifelessly at the sky.

"What do I do?" Kia said quietly to herself as tears began to fill her eyes. This was not the way her birthday was supposed to end and she was certain that the taxi driver hadn't anticipated such a final end to his evening either.

Unable to do anything else Kia took hold of the driver's hand gently and closed her eyes. It didn't seem right to just leave him.

She didn't notice the burning sensation in her palm at first as her body was already full of aches from the collision but after a few minutes it was impossible to ignore and her eyes shot open to look down at the hand that held onto that of the driver. Kia wasn't certain but she thought she could see a strange white glow around their hands and then, as quickly as it started, the pain faded away and seconds later so did the glow.

Shaking her head to clear her thoughts Kia decided she was imagining things due to the stress of the accident.

Then the driver began to cough.

"What happened?" He asked, rubbing his free hand over his face as he straightened the leg that moments ago had seemed irrevocably broken.

"Accident," Kia said, unable to form any more coherent words than that, relief flooding her body at the sound of the ambulance sirens rapidly approaching.

***

Kia had been glad to let the paramedics lead her away from the taxi driver, wrapping a blue woollen blanket around her shoulders and telling her she was probably in shock.

Sofia and Rebekah were already seated on the curb wrapped in matching blankets and Kia joined them without comment as they sat and watched one of the paramedics checking over the taxi driver while another assessed the driver of the other vehicle.

It was almost unbelievable as the taxi driver got to his feet, shaking his head as he refused the paramedics insistence that they put him on a stretcher.

"I'm fine," Kia heard him saying, "I don't know how but I'm fine."

Kia remembered little of the journey to the hospital or the cursory examination she received before being declared uninjured, her mind seemed to have hit pause, unable to think clearly as she tried to rationalise what had happened.

"Mum?" Kia said as her mother answered the phone. "Mum I don't want you to panic... everyone is all right."

"What's happened?" Katherine asked, fear gripping at her chest, no one told you not to panic unless they were about to tell you something that they assumed would make you panic.

"We've had a bit of an accident…"

"Are you hurt?"

"Didn't I just say everyone is all right?"

"What about Sofia and Rebekah?"

"Everyone mum, everyone is all right."

"You promise me?"

"Yeah, I swear."

"What happened?"

"I'm not really sure, the taxi we were in hit another car…"

"But you're all right?"

"Mum!"

"Sorry…"

"We're at the hospital, can you come and get me?"

"Of course I can sweetheart," Katherine said, already struggling into her jacket without moving the phone from her ear, "I'll be right there."

"And mum… something happened…"

"What sort of something?"

"You know…" Kia looked around to see if she was likely to be overheard. "The thing we were talking about earlier… I mean I could be wrong… but I think I… I think I just found out what my gift is."

"Don't move honey, I'm on my way."

Chapter Nine

Kia cradled a hot cup of tea, letting the steam rise up into her face and ease the strange chill that seemed to have settled into her bones.

Katherine had taken no time at all getting to the hospital, only bringing her daughter back home once she had been certain that Kia had been given the all clear. The girl was visibly shaken but Katherine knew not all of that was down to the accident. Asking Sofia and Rebekah if they needed taking home, Katherine was relieved when they both refused as their own parents were already on the way. As much as she liked her daughter's friends, at that moment, Katherine needed some time alone with Kia.

"Are you ready to tell me yet?" Katherine asked. Kia had been silent the whole journey home, barely even making a sound to accept the offer of a cup of tea.

"I don't know," Kia said quietly, sipping at her drink before wincing at the unexpected sweetness. "Sugar?"

"It's good for shock."

"It's horrible." Kia smiled as she put the drink down on the coffee table. "Thanks for coming for me."

"What else was I going to do? I'm just so relieved you weren't hurt... I hope the police are going to investigate what the hell happened... that man shouldn't be allowed to drive people around if he can't control his own vehicle... and then he gets away with hardly a scratch!"

"Mum that's the thing," Kia said, rubbing at the palm of her hand as she remembered the burning sensation.

"What's the thing?"

"I don't think he did get away with hardly a scratch."

"Of course he did... I saw him... walking about large as life as if he hadn't just put my daughter's life in danger."

"But... he..."

"What Kia? What is it?"

"When I first got to him... he was hurt... badly... I think, I think maybe he was dead..."

"Don't be silly how could he..." Katherine stopped, her eyes widening as the realisation hit her. "Kia what did you do?"

"I don't know... I just held his hand and wished that he was okay... and then... and then he sort of was..."

"Oh my... I... your Grandma told me stories of... but I never thought..."

"What? Never thought what? Mum what am I?"

"I think you may well be one of the most blessed of all Assaie's daughters..."

"What do you mean?"

"I think you're a healer." Katherine couldn't hide the amazement from her face as she looked at her daughter. Was it really possible that her little girl had been given the most precious of all Assaie's gifts? "You remember Assaie's child with Jacob?"

"Yeah, Althaia wasn't it?"

"That's her... she was the first to be gifted and she was a healer... but since then it has been so rare... my mother had only been told of one other to have such abilities, until now."

***

Kia looked at herself in the mirror. She looked the same as she did only a couple of days before, same hair, same eyes, same girl looking back at her and yet she was completely different.

She had always assumed there would be some kind of feeling of being "grown up" when she hit eighteen but she had no idea exactly what that was going to mean for her. How could she have even guessed at the news her mother would break to her that morning, how her life would change so dramatically? She had no idea how her mother had managed to keep such a secret for eighteen years.

Yawning widely Kia rubbed her eyes. Her sleep had been fitful at best, filled with dreams of car crashes and Goddesses, of death and life, and in the middle of it all a blue-grey eyed young man smiling and telling her everything was going to be okay.

"Kia you awake?" Katherine said quietly at Kia's bedroom door, not wanting to wake the girl if she was still sleeping.

"Yeah, come in," Kia said, turning around on her dressing table stool to face the door as her mother entered.

"How you feeling?" Katherine asked, perching on the edge of Kia's bed as she looked her daughter over. "You look tired. Have you slept at all?"

"Some, I just kept having odd dreams."

"Did you dream of Assaie?"

"Yeah, how did you know?"

"I did the night I learned of her, your Grandma did to... I think maybe that's another part of it."

"You could have warned me," Kia said, covering her mouth to stifle a yawn and failing. "Do you remember what you dreamt?"

"Like it was yesterday." Katherine smiled a little wistfully as she remembered the dream in which the Goddess had spoken to her. It might have only been a dream but it had felt so much more, and even so many years later Katherine could feel the same comfort and strength she had taken from Assaie's words. "She told me that I was loved and that I was special and if I gave it time I would learn the true blessing of the gift I had been given."

"She said almost the same to me," Kia said, moving from the stool to sit beside her mother and rest her head on Katherine's shoulder.

"Almost?" Katherine said slightly surprised, "What was different."

"She told me that I had to learn the limits of my gift and that some things are not meant to be healed, some deaths are natural and are meant to be."

Slipping her arm around Kia's shoulder Katherine held her daughter tightly. She had been proud of the girl since the day she was born and nothing had ever dissuaded her of that, but now that pride was beyond measure. All of Assaie's daughter's were special but Katherine's was even more so.

"Mum?" Kia said after a while, sitting upright to look her mother in the face.

"Yes sweetheart?"

"Was it hard? Knowing what was to come for me, what you had to let me know in time but having to keep it a secret?"

"Not hard as such," Katherine said, her lips pursed as she thought best how to explain. "It's not like it was always on my mind, I mean I thought of it sometimes, when you were born and I suppose each birthday as it got closer but it was never a bad thing... you'll understand when you have a daughter of your own."

"What if I don't?" Kia asked, suddenly curious about how this inheritance of hers could be affected if she didn't have a child. "I might not have kids ... or I could have a boy... would he get the gift too?"

"You'll have a daughter," Katherine said with a confident smile. "We all do."

"What do you mean?"

"I suppose you could say it's another part of who we are; we always have a girl... just the one... just like Assaie had."

"But what if something happened to that girl? What then?"

"It never has, I don't know how but I think perhaps Assaie looks over us, protects us..."

Kia yawned, wider than ever, stretching her arms up to the ceiling in an attempt to ease the stiffness in her shoulders.

"You should get back to bed," Katherine said, getting to her feet, "Get some more sleep, it looks like you need it."

"Yeah maybe," Kia yawned again, her eyes opening wide as she remembered. "I'm meant to be going out tonight... I was going to go shopping with Sof for a new dress or something..."

"I don't think that's such a good idea after last night do you? Going out with who?"

"With everything that happened I totally forgot to tell you," Kia's grin was wide and enthusiastic as she spoke. "Mum, I met a boy... he's really cute... and nice... and funny, not as funny as he thinks but still... and he asked me out on a date!"

"In that case," Katherine said, pulling back the duvet on Kia's bed and ushering her daughter beneath it. "I suggest you get some sleep so you don't go on your big date with dark rings under your eyes, and then you can tell me all about this boy later."

"But a new dress?"

"You have plenty of dresses, I'm sure something in that vast wardrobe of yours will do just fine."

Kia took a breath to argue but the truth was she was far too tired to go shopping, even for clothes and her bed was just far too comfortable and inviting. She was already asleep before Katherine had left her room.

Kia awoke with a jump as her mobile phone danced its vibratory dance on her bedside table, bleary eyed she grabbed for it and squinted at the screen to see who would be calling her so early. The display told her two things, firstly Sophia was calling her and secondly it was two o'clock in the afternoon.

"K. Are you alright?" Sophia asked as soon as Kia answered.

"Yeah, had a bad night... mum made me go back to bed. How are you doing?"

"Same, nightmares you know... that was some scary stuff last night... I was so sure the taxi driver was going to be dead."

"Yeah, yeah me too..."

"Don't think I've ever been so freaked out in my life!"

"How did your folks deal with it?" Kia asked knowing that of all their parents Sofia's were the most over protective.

"Pretty much how you would imagine, dad wants to wrap me up in cotton wool and mum thinks I should go to counselling!"

"So business as usual then?"

Sofia laughed softly. "Yeah."

"You spoken to Rebs?"

"She called me just before I called you, hangover from hell as you'd expect after last night but other than that she's okay."

"Good, I'll text her in a bit."

"So... you still seeing Mr. Handsome later?"

"I dunno, I guess so..."

"You don't sound keen?"

"Oh I am... course I am but you know, after last night, I just don't know if it's a good idea..."

"K we could have all been badly hurt last night, or worse... if that's not a good enough reason to enjoy life I don't know what is!"

"Yeah, yeah you're right," Kia said, throwing her duvet to one side and swinging her legs out of the bed. "I'd better get going Sof, I'll call you later, or tomorrow..."

"Speak to you later K, and have a good time!"

The soothing therapeutic heat of the shower helped Kia begin to feel a little more human and the extra sleep had taken away the exhaustion she had felt earlier. Letting the water flow over her face Kia tried to recall the dreams she had had when she'd gone back to sleep but they were all a hazy blur, the details slipping away like the water swirling and gurgling down the drain.

Finally and reluctantly getting out of the shower Kia wrapped her hair in a towel before pulling on her dressing gown, she could already hear her mother pottering about in the kitchen, probably making a light lunch for whenever Kia finally surfaced.

"Are they for me?" Kia asked as she nodded at a plate of sandwiches on the side.

"Well hello sleepy head," Katherine said glad to see her daughter looking more refreshed than the last time she had seen her. "You look better, and yes, if you want them."

"Any chance of a cuppa?" Kia said, grabbing one of the cheese and pickle sandwiches and taking a large bite. "No sugar this time."

Sitting down at the small breakfast bar while Katherine made two mugs of tea Kia quickly demolished the plate of sandwiches, surprised at the extent of her appetite as she looked around to see what else might be available.

"There's some crisps in the cupboard if you're still hungry," Katherine said over her shoulder, demonstrating her knack, or was that gift, for knowing just what her daughter was feeling.

Helping herself to some crisps Kia happily crunched her way through them, reaching for her tea and taking a quick sip as soon as it was placed before her.

"So come on then," Katherine said, taking the seat facing her daughter. "Tell me all about this boy you've met."

"Oh mum he's lovely... his name is Xander and he's so yummy... and he asked me out... Me! Not Rebs or Sof..."

"So he's got good taste at least," Katherine said smiling at her daughter's obvious excitement. "And where is he planning on taking you?"

"Oh… he said a meal… but I dunno where…"

"So how are you going to get there?"

"We're meant to be meeting outside the cinema on King Street… you don't mind me going out again do you? I mean after last night…"

"That's hardly going to happen again is it? Besides I can't go forbidding you to go out… you're not my little girl any more."

Finishing her tea Kia got to her feet and walked around the breakfast bar to give her mother a hug.

"I'll always be your little girl mum," she said before heading out of the kitchen, she still had an outfit to choose and didn't see her mother wiping a tear from her eye as she watched Kia leave the room.

Chapter Ten

Every one of Xander's shirts was strewn across his bed, each having been tried on and then subsequently rejected. Stripes, checks, plain; nothing seemed quite right.

Looking at himself in the mirror attached to his wardrobe door Xander's brow furrowed. Wearing nothing but his best black jeans Xander began to question even that choice. Perhaps he should wear trousers? Were jeans too casual? Did they not give out the right message?

What message *could* a pair of jeans give in the first place? Would it look like he didn't care, hadn't made an effort, but then again what if he wore his good trousers, would it look like he was trying too hard then?

With a heavy sigh Xander sat down on his bed with a thud and buried his face in his hands. Getting ready for a date had never been this hard before. Normally his choice of clothing came down to grabbing the first clean and ironed shirt that his hand hit when he reached into the wardrobe, but nothing about this date felt normal; certainly not the colony of butterflies which seemed to have taken up residence inside his stomach.

"Knock, knock..."

Xander raised his head as his mother's face appeared around the corner of his bedroom door.

"Everything all right up here?" Xander's mother asked as she entered his room, shaking her head slightly as she took in the mess. Her son's room was rarely spotless but the pile of shirts on the bed made it look even more untidy than usual. "You've been stomping about up here for an hour now."

Sitting down on the bed Xander's mother nudged him gently, her hand reaching up to ruffle his hair, an action that she knew would drive him mad as his own hand quickly shot up to correct the mess she had made, but she couldn't resist the small display of affection that she had used since he was a boy. Smoothing back his hair Xander smiled, the truth was he would miss the day she finally thought him too old for such an act.

"Want to tell me what's up?"

Suzanna Matthews was a slight woman, both her husband and son towering over her in stature, but her quiet nature and gentle manner hid an inner strength that the two men had often come to rely on. As she smiled at her only child, the pride of her life, the edges of her pale blue eyes crinkled. Over the years, Suzanna had noticed the few lines on her face growing in number and becoming a little more pronounced, but she saw no reason to worry as her face merely reflected the passing years and the lines around her eyes were testimony to the countless hours she spent smiling. Not one to bother much with make-up, and when she did it was always to enhance rather than hide her natural looks, Suzanna had an elegant beauty that was often overlooked due to her simple style of dress and the way she nearly always wore her long brown hair, now beginning to pepper with silver, in a basic pony tail.

However, when she did have cause to dress up for an evening out, she still had the power to turn heads and take the breath away of both her husband and son.

George Matthews on the other hand could never be described as anything other than classically handsome, his jet black hair and deep brown eyes could have easily belonged to any 1940's movie start, while his broad shoulders and tall stature made him a formidable sight. Being a decade older than his wife, George's hair was now more-grey than black and his looks had settled into that of a mature gentleman but one glimpse of his wife could still start his heart racing in a way that his son was only just beginning to understand.

"I have no idea what to wear," Xander said with an exaggerated sigh that made his mother chuckle softly, having no daughters that was a phrase Suzanna had never expected to hear from her child.

"You have a wardrobe full of shirts... well right now you have a bed full of them!"

"But they're not right..."

"What's wrong with them?"

"I don't know... none of them seem good enough..."

"So who is this girl that has managed to get my son in such a fluster?" Suzanna asked as she got to her feet and began to gather up the shirts from Xander's bed, placing each one on its hanger and returning it to the wardrobe until a single plain deep blue shirt remained.

"Just a girl," Xander said with a shrug, taking up the shirt his mother had left and slipping it on. "But..."

"But?"

"I dunno... she just seems... different... special..."

Suzanna smiled and nodded her approval as Xander turned to face her, his shirt done up save for the top button.

"Tie?" Xander asked, already feeling more confident in his attire.

"Too formal," Suzanna advised.

"Trainers?"

"Shoes… and clean them."

"Thanks mum," Xander said, bending down to press a kiss of gratitude to Suzanna's cheek.

"Alexander… if this girl is so special you make sure you treat her right."

"Mum!"

"No one night stand and then never calling."

"Mum!" Xander's voice went up an octave and his cheeks went a deep red.

"What? You think I don't know what young men are like? Your dad and I were young once too you know."

"But still…"

"What? You'd rather I pretend I still think my son plays with Lego?"

"Yes please!"

"Oh and Alexander…"

"Yes mum?"

"You look very handsome… she's a lucky girl."

"Thanks mum." Looking at his watch Xander grimaced.

"Where are you meeting her?" Suzanna asked, poised to offer her son a lift if his extended preparations for the evening had left him running late.

"Outside King Street cinema."

"Oh that's only a ten minute walk away... What time do you need to be there?"

"In an hour and a half!"

*

Xander had been waiting outside the cinema as Kia's car, driven by her mother, pulled up across the road. The car stopped and the two women watched him for a moment. He was obviously unsure of which direction she would come from and he kept looking this way and that before checking his watch and reaching up to adjust a tie that wasn't there.

Kia couldn't hold back her giggles, he really did look adorably cute.

"He is very handsome," Katherine said echoing her daughter's thoughts.

"Thanks for bringing me mum."

"Don't be silly, and if you want me to pick you up just call."

Kia smiled and gratefully kissed Katherine on the cheek before moving to get out of the car, they both knew what she had meant, if Kia felt too nervous to call a taxi.

"I'll be fine," Kia said, leaning back into the car.

"Have a good time sweetheart."

"Thanks mum. Love you."

"Love you too, now go and put that young man out of his misery!"

Slamming the car door closed Kia took a deep breath and crossed the road to where her date was waiting. It wasn't as if she had never dated before but she had never felt this nervous. Something told Kia that Xander was someone special.

"Hi," Xander said as Kia approached, his smile wide but a little shy, his hand automatically going to his hair in a nervous gesture that already seemed familiar.

He looked good. His skin was smooth and fresh, obviously freshly shaved and Kia could get the hint of a subtle aftershave as she got closer. He was dressed in plain black jeans and a deep blue shirt left open at the collar, his black shoes shining in the fading August sunshine.

"Hi yourself," Kia said smiling, resisting the urge to check her own hair and instead linked her hands together to stop them from carrying on without conscious thought.

Leaning forward Xander kissed Kia's cheek gently. It was barely a brush of his lips against her skin, an awkward nervous action and yet somehow it set Kia's skin of fire. She felt her face flush and she looked down at her feet to hide her embarrassment.

"I'm so glad you could make it tonight," Xander said, either not noticing or gallantly ignoring Kia's bashfulness. "I mean I would have understood after last night..."

"Well, no one was hurt, we were all just shaken up a bit... besides I was looking forward to coming."

"You were?"

"Of course."

"Right. Good... you look beautiful by the way."

"I don't know about that," Kia said blushing and smoothing down her dress. "I was going to get something new but after last night it wasn't really possible."

"Well I'm glad you didn't because you look perfect in that."

Kia silently thanked her mother for insisting that the simple but elegant summer dress with a delicate floral design was the perfect choice for the evening, coupled with low heels and matching clutch bag Kia looked like someone who had made the effort, but not too much.

Kia smiled again, desperately trying to think of something to say she absent mindedly twisted her new silver bangle around her wrist, opening her mouth a fraction only to close it a second later when no words came to mind. Inside her head she could hear her own voice screaming at her. "Say something will you… he's going to think you're a right idiot!"

"We'd better get going," Xander said, finally breaking the awkward silence, "Our reservation is in ten minutes."

"Yeah… where are we going? You never said."

"Just a quiet little place a couple of blocks away if that's okay… it's pretty good, decent food."

"Great, lead the way."

Xander grinned and brazenly took hold of Kia's hand, his grip both firm and gentle and his touch once again setting Kia's skin on fire.

"This way," he said setting off, his grip giving Kia no option but to follow him, not that she wouldn't have gladly followed him to the ends of the earth at that moment.

The walk to the restaurant only took a few minutes and, as they walked, the conversation began to grow more relaxed and their initial nerves faded into a more manageable background excitement.

"So how is that friend of yours after last night? She seemed pretty wasted in the club… can't imagine the accident helped her feel any better."

"Actually I think she probably got off lighter than the rest of us."

"Oh?"

"She was already that relaxed that she didn't tense up when we crashed. Sof has got some terrible bruising where the seatbelt was. I think the worse Rebs had was a shocking hangover."

"What about you? You weren't hurt?"

"Couple of bruises but nothing to worry about."

"Good, I'm glad," Xander came to a halt outside a discreet restaurant that Kia hadn't noticed. "Here we are," he said pushing the door open and holding it for Kia to enter before him.

The restaurant was small but warm and friendly looking and the waitress greeted them with a bright smile as Xander told her they had a reservation. Without stopping to check in the reservations book the waitress led them over to a quiet table in the corner of the room.

Once they were seated the waitress handed them the menus before asking if they wanted anything to drink.

"What do you fancy," Xander asked, already having decided that he would let Kia decide if the evening was to include alcohol or not.

"Erm, Samos Anthemis?"

"Make it a bottle," Xander said with a smile.

Once the waitress had left them Kia allowed herself time to look around the room. The décor, in muted shades of reds, seemed a little dated and the tea lights in the middle of each table was perhaps a touch chintzy but the overall feeling of the place was of comfort, friends and good food. Kia decided she liked it.

"So what do you think?" Xander asked after Kia had looked around for a while.

"Seems nice," Kia said honestly. "Hope the food is as good."

"It is."

"You've been before?"

"Yeah, yeah you could say that..."

"How do you mean?"

"Well actually... it's my folks place."

"Really?" Kia laughed softly, "I am so glad I didn't say I hated it now!"

"I know it's probably not the trendiest of places but... well you seemed the sort of person who understands that substance is more important than packaging."

"It looks like a nice place," Kia said looking around the room again until her eyes came to rest on the door that lead to the kitchen. "Your folks aren't through there waiting to check me out are they?"

"No," Xander said, his voice tinkling with a small laugh, "At least they'd better not be it's their night off."

Kia smiled before turning her attention to the menu to hide her unexpected relief. It was somewhat early to be at the "meet the parents" stage of the relationship.

"They do a good steak," Xander suggested, the tone of his voice making it quite apparent that his choice of food was already pre-selected before they had even arrived.

"Hmm no," Kia said crinkling her nose as the suggestion. "Think I'll try the Two Cheese, Spinach and Cashew Nut Pasta."

"Oh? Oh! Are you vegetarian?"

"Not... not as such, I mean not in any decided or conscious way I wouldn't say... I just don't like meat... or the idea of eating it..."

"Shit, sorry, I don't have to have the steak... I can have something else."

"Don't be silly," Kia said shaking her head. "You have what you want... you don't have to change your eating habits for me."

"I know I don't have to, but I want to. What about a starter?"

"I never usually bother... to be honest I'd rather save room for a dessert later."

"Ah a girl after my own heart," Xander said, closing the menus as the waitress returned with their wine. "We'll have two of the Two Cheese, Spinach and Cashew Nut Pasta."

By the raising of the waitresses eyebrows Kia knew that the woman had never known Xander to order anything other than steak before and, although the gesture was unnecessary, it was nonetheless appreciated.

Wine glasses filled they faced each other, quiet again. Despite thinking that the tea lights were a little tacky Kia couldn't deny they ambience they had given the room, Xander looked particularly appealing in the flickering candle light.

"Did I mention how lovely you look?" Xander asked, knowing full well that he had but enjoying the flush of pink that coloured Kia's cheeks.

"I think you have," Kia replied, picking up her wine glass and taking a sip so that she didn't have to look him in the eye for a few seconds.

"Well I meant it," Xander said once Kia's gaze had returned to his face. "Seriously, I think you might possibly be the most beautiful girl I've ever seen."

"Stop it," Kia said, the soft pink of her cheeks turning a deep crimson.

"But I mean it."

"You're embarrassing me."

"I don't see why, people must tell you how beautiful you are all the time."

"Only my mum!"

"Well then your mother is a very clever woman."

Seeing that Kia was getting uncomfortable with his compliments Xander changed the subject and their conversation turned to more mundane topics. Kia spoke of her college course in health care and thoughts of maybe one day going into nursing or child care, while Xander spoke enthusiastically about his job in a local garage.

"So you're a mechanic?"

"Much to my parents dismay... but cooking was just never me... trust me, I could burn water."

"At least I know where to come when I have car trouble."

"Oh what do you have?"

"A mini, black... she's gorgeous!"

Xander chuckled.

"What?" Kia asked, slightly distracted by his dimple as he smiled.

"I've never understood that whole 'she' thing with cars."

"I dunno," Kia said with a shrug. "She just looks like a she. She's too pretty to be a he!"

"I bet you've named her too."

"Now you're teasing me."

"You have haven't you?"

"I might have."

"Well?"

"I'm not telling you now," Kia said with an exaggerated pout, "You'll only laugh at me."

"I won't, I promise."

"Promise?"

"Cross my heart," Xander said making the gesture across his chest.

"Mimi."

Xander burst out laughing the second the name was said.

"Hey you promised," Kia said with a scowl that she couldn't keep up for long before she was laughing with him.

"I know," Xander said apologetically, "But really... Mimi the mini?"

Once the food arrived the conversation waned as they ate, Xander surprised at how much he was enjoying his non-steak meal.

"This is really good," Kia said once her plate was half empty. "We'll definitely have to come here again."

"So there will be again?"

"Well... I hope so... if you want of course."

"Yeah, yeah I really do."

***

Once their meal, and dessert, had been consumed and the wine bottle drunk dry Xander suggested they go for a walk.

The night was still warm as they headed towards the town's small but pretty park. The sun had set but it was still far from being dark and they walked comfortably in silence, hand in hand, arms swinging as they moved.

As they walked down the gravel path that ran through the centre of the park their feet made a satisfying crunching sound and Xander began to stomp, making the sound louder.

"What are you doing?" Kia asked with a laugh.

"I don't really know," Xander said, dropping her hand and he stomped ahead before turning around to face her, his feet still crunching hard on the gravel. "I used to do this as a kid, I've always like the noise."

"I think you might be a little bit crazy."

"Oh I think you might be right. But that's a good thing isn't it?"

"We shall see." Drawing up beside a small wooden bench Kia stopped. "Come on noisy boy, come and sit down."

"As you wish," Xander said, bowing deeply before joining her on the bench.

The sat quietly, enjoying the calm evening air and the pleasure of just being together.

"I am glad you agreed to come out with me," Xander said after a while, his tone serious and lacking any of its earlier teasing quality.

"So am I... I'm glad you asked."

"I couldn't not... I was nervous you'd turn me down... that's why I was so... you know... stupid."

"You were a little..."

"You're not meant to agree with that!"

"Sorry."

"Kia..."

"Yes?"

Xander's hand touched Kia's face lightly, moving over her cheek, his fingers sinking into her hair as he leaned forward.

Kia's heart began to race as she felt his breath on her face, moving as if in slow motion ever closer until his lips were touching hers. The fire she had felt at the touch of his kiss at the start of their date was nothing in comparison to the inferno that was now ignited in her.

Leaning into the kiss Kia's arms reached to pull Xander against her, pressing their bodies closer together as their kiss intensified, an explosion of fireworks going off in both of their minds until they finally parted, breathless and somewhat stunned.

"Wow," Xander said, unable to think of any other coherent word, which was slightly better than Kia had fared having temporarily lost the power of speech.

Chapter Eleven

"So come on, tell us everything!" Sofia bounced excitedly on Kia's bed hungry for the gossip of her friend's first date with Xander.

"And don't leave anything out," Rebekah added with a mischievous grin and lascivious wink.

"Nothing like that happened Rebekah!" Kia said, turning her head with mock affront and picking up her cup of tea to sip slowly. "I don't know what kind of girl you think I am!"

"Well from what Sof tells me he's pretty damn hot so it's not like we'd blame you," Rebekah said, her grin growing even wider and more mischievous.

"If you hadn't been so wasted the other night you would have seen how hot he is," Sofia said pointedly.

"Well if I hadn't been they might not have met so I think it all worked out just how it was supposed to actually!"

"Nah," Kia said, putting down her tea, "We would have met somehow… we couldn't not."

"Oh it sounds like a case of the L word to me," Sofia teased, pushing her friend gently.

"It's too early to be saying that but…"

"But?"

"I dunno there's just... something... it feels like we were always meant to be."

"Fate," Sofia said.

"Destiny," Rebekah agreed. "So what happened?"

Settling back against her headboard as if holding court Kia smiled wildly at her friends as she prepared to relate the events of the night before. She loved having friends she could share everything with. Kia paused as the thought crossed her mind, could she really share everything with them? Everything?

"Come on," Sofia prompted, "Spill!"

"Right okay," Kia began before giving her friends a blow by blow account of her date, Sofia and Rebekah ohh-ing and ahh-ing in all the right places, enjoying experiencing Kia's new found romance however vicariously. "And then he kissed me," Kia concluded, her face the image of bliss as she recalled the feeling of Xander's lips against hers.

"How was it?" Sofia asked breathlessly.

"Good," Kia said, searching for the necessary words to describe something that had transported her out of her own body.

"Just good?" Sofia said, "We need more than that... was it soft?"

"Wet?" Prompted Rebekah, "Hard... passionate... did he use his tongue?"

"It was... it was like I didn't know what it was to be kissed until that moment... it felt like my whole brain just exploded and fireworks went off through my whole body... I don't think I have ever been so sorry for something to stop in my whole life."

"Wow," Sofia said, slumping against the wall at the side of the bed.

"I want a Xander," Rebekah said slouching against her friend as they commiserated each other for not having such passion in their lives.

Kia couldn't help but smile, seeing her friends reactions just enhanced what she already knew was an amazing experience. She had been walking on clouds from the moment Xander had kissed her and still hadn't stopped. Kia had been on such a high that she hadn't even had a moment of concern as he said goodnight to her by seeing her into a taxi. Rather than worrying about the previous night's terrible experience all that Kia had been able to think about was the moment she would see him again. The car had barely pulled away from the kerb before he had sent a text thanking her for a perfect evening and telling her, yet again, just how beautiful she was.

"He is quite something," Kia said with a rather wistful smile, grabbing her phone to quickly scroll through her photographs until she got to the one she had taken of the two of them sitting on the park bench.

"You do make a gorgeous couple," Rebekah said craning her neck to peer at the photograph. "He's just dreamy isn't he?"

"You're not wrong," Kia said, her heart swelling as she looked as his picture. He was gorgeous and smart and funny and everything a girl could want and best of all he liked her.

"You're so lucky," Sofia said, her tone somehow managing to sound both envious and pleased. It wasn't that she didn't want her friend to have such happiness in her life, but Sofia couldn't help but wonder if and when it would be her turn to find herself someone so seemingly perfect.

"I really am," Kia agreed, reluctantly putting her phone to one side. She really had to get that picture printed off to put by her bed. "I can't believe just how much my life has changed in the last couple of days... what with Xander and..."

"And what?" Rebekah asked, she was not aware of any other momentous occasions happing in her friend's life.

"And... you know... turning eighteen..." Kia stammered, her words not convincing even to herself.

"What else Miss Deering?" Sofia said, looking closely at her friend, her gaze unwavering as Kia tried to avoid direct eye contact.

Kia swallowed wondering if she dared and knowing she would probably implode if she didn't. The three friends hadn't kept secrets from each other since swearing their pact when they were just thirteen and she had the biggest secret ever to share now.

"Wait here a minute," Kia said, getting from the bed and leaving the room.

Sofia and Rebekah looked at each other and shrugged, neither having a clue about what their friend might be keeping from them.

A couple of minutes later Kia returned with a large bread knife in her hand to the raised eyebrows and questioning looks of her friends.

"Here," Kia said offering the knife to Sofia.

"What?" Sofia asked without reaching to take the knife.

"Take it," Kia insisted, "Cut your hand with it."

"Yeah right," Sofia said, looking at her friend as if she had lost her mind, "Because that is something I'm going to do."

"Go on, please... you'll understand why when I show you..."

"Err how about no!"

In a quick movement Kia grabbed for Sofia's hand and ran the blade across her palm before she could stop her, the blood quickly pooling as Kia grabbed some tissues to stop it spilling on her duvet.

"Are you insane?" Sofia said, snatching her hand back, her eyes wide in shock and pain.

"Trust me, it'll be OK," Kia said pulling Sofia's hand back and holding it tightly in her own.

Closing her eyes tightly Kia concentrated, the now more familiar burning sensation ignited her palm joined by a gentle glow and then Kia let go. "There," she announced with satisfaction.

Looking at her hand Sofia couldn't quite understand. There was still a smear of blood but no wound that had been there only moments before. It didn't make sense.

"So what was that?" Sofia asked. "Some kind of trick knife?"

"Trick knife?" Kia echoed incredulously. "How could that be a trick knife?"

"You know," Sofia said with a shrug, "One of those ones that looks like it cuts but doesn't, it just leaves a trail of fake blood."

"But you felt it cut you?"

"Yeah but you know how the mind can fool us sometimes, we think something should hurt so it does!"

"It's not a trick knife!"

"Do me!" Rebekah said stretching out her hand, curious to see how this trick worked.

With a slightly disheartened shrug Kia picked up the bread knife again. She had rather expected her friends to react with amazement and wonder, not assume it was some sort of parlour trick.

With a swift movement she scored a deep cut through Rebekah's palm.

"Ouch!" Rebekah squealed before looking closely at the cut. The blood looked real enough and as she moved her hand the cut across the middle of her palm gaped. There was no mistaking it was real. "You just cut me!"

"You asked me to."

"But I didn't think it was real, Sof said it was a trick."

"Here," Kia said taking a tight hold of Rebekah's hand and once again closing her eyes. Once more there was the heat and the light and then Rebekah's skin was as unmarked as it had been when she first entered the room.

"It's gone," Rebekah said, her tone now filled with awe as she tried to find some evidence of the deep cut that had seconds ago scored the middle of her hand. "How is it gone? What did you do?"

"It's a long story," Kia said, pleased that the idea of a trick seemed to have been overcome.

"Hang on," Sofia said taking hold of Kia's hand and turning it over to reveal the image of the goddess pendant scorched into her palm. "What's that?"

"It's... I suppose you could call it a birth mark," Kia said, taking her hand back and rubbing the mark that still tingled.

"We've known you for years Kia," Sofia said, "And I have never once seen you with a birthmark... so what is it really?"

"Okay it's more of a... I don't know... I suppose you could call it a re-birth mark."

"But what did you do?" Rebekah asked again, her tone less in awe and more in concern.

"It's all right Rebs, I just healed it," Kia said, reaching to hold her friend's hand but it was quickly snatched away from her.

"Just healed it?" Rebekah repeated. "What do you mean JUST healed it … K there is no just about healing something… what… what the hell are you?"

"I'm me… like I've always been… Kia."

"The Kia I've always known couldn't go around magically healing things … what are you? Like some kind of witch?"

"No of course not… Rebs calm down."

"Calm down?" Rebekah said as she got off the bed and began to back towards the bedroom door, stumbling as she went but she couldn't take her eyes off Kia for fear of what she might do.

"Rebs you're over reacting." Sofia said kindly, she was finding it all a bit overwhelming too but they could always count on Rebekah to take her reactions to the extreme.

"You think?" Rebekah said, reaching behind her to open the door. "How the hell do we know what she just did to us? We could be infected or anything…"

"Infected with what?"

"I don't know… magic stuff… you really want to hang around to find out?"

"Rebs really, come on." Kia got off the bed and took a few steps towards Rebekah, stopping when her friend held her hands out in front of her.

"Stay away witch," Rebekah said as she backed out of the bedroom before running down the stairs and out of the front door, barely giving herself time to open it first.

"She'll be okay," Sofia said with a kind smile as Kia turned away from the door and moved back to her bed, her earlier bright expression replaced with dismay. "You know Rebs, she reacts before she thinks. Just give her time to calm down."

"She was scared of me."

"You've got to admit K, this was quite a bombshell you've just dropped on us... I mean... what the hell?"

"I know, I just... you two are my best friends in the whole world... if I can't tell you things then who can I?"

"There are things and then there are THINGS... and then there is the sudden ability to heal people? I say sudden unless you've always been able to do this?"

"No not always," Kia said, grateful that at least one of her close friends had been willing to hear the full story. "Just a couple of days now... to be honest I wasn't a hundred percent sure it would work just now."

"But you cut me anyway? Thanks mate!"

"I assumed it would, I mean it was only a small cut and after the taxi driver..."

"The taxi driver?" Sofia's face darkened with concern. "What about the taxi driver?"

"Well you know how the paramedics said it was a miracle he wasn't badly hurt?"

"Yeah," Sofia felt her skin begin to prickle, she had a horrible feeling she knew what Kia was about to tell her and she wasn't completely sure she wanted to hear it.

"Well, when I got to him, he was... very badly in fact..."

"How badly?"

"I'm not certain," Kia's voice dropped to a low whisper. "I think maybe he was dead."

"And you..?"

"Yeah..."

"Okay...okay..." Sofia got to her feet, her hands running aimlessly through her hair as she tried to reconcile this new information with the girl she had known for so many years. "He was dead?"

"Yeah."

"And then he wasn't?"

"Well... yeah..."

"Kia?"

"Yes Sof?"

"What the hell are you?"

****

Kia had never experienced such conflicting emotions at the same time before. Her friends' reactions had left her devastated. Although Sofia had not raced from the house in the same way Rebekah had her reaction had, nevertheless, been one of fear and she had made her excuses to leave as soon as she could.

Kia had relied on the support of her two best friends for so many years and the three of them had always been so close that she had, mistakenly, believed they would have been excited by her new found ability or at the very least that they would have given her the time to explain, but instead they fled from her as if she were something grotesque and terrifying.

Katherine had heard the front door slamming closed twice and instantly knew that something was wrong. Her daughter had flown into her arm the second she entered Kia's bedroom, sobbing so uncontrollably that it took a while for Katherine to get the full story out of her. Rocking Kia in her arms and making soothing sounds Katherine assured the girl that everything would be all right and that her friends would just need some time to digest this new information they had discovered about their friend. In her heart however Katherine was afraid that Kia had just lost the support of people who she would need by her side as she learned what her gift could cost her.

"They were afraid of me mum, like I was some sort of monster or something..."

"I know sweetheart."

"But they know me, how could they be like that? I thought we could cope with anything the three of us, like we always have."

"You have to admit Kia, this is something a little out of the ordinary. You need to understand what a shock this has been to them, you need to give them time to work it out themselves, and hope that they don't go around telling anyone."

"Telling anyone?" The thought had never even crossed Kia's mind. "Do you think they might?"

"I don't know. It's possible."

"Would that be such a bad thing?"

"Think about it sweetheart, Rebekah and Sofia are your closest friends and look how they reacted... how do you think strangers would take this?"

"I shouldn't have told them should I?" Kia said, burying her face in Katherine's shoulder and taking the comfort of her mother's arms holding her tightly.

"It was a risk," Katherine agreed, "But you could never know how they would react, there's no point beating yourself up about it now. We'll just have to hope they calm down in a couple of days yeah?"

"Yeah I guess."

Kia sighed, the elation she had been feeling over the last couple of days was gone and she was utterly deflated.

Just when she thought she might crawl under her duvet and stay there for the rest of her life Kia's mobile phone beeped, alerting her to a new text message.

Kia grabbed for the phone hoping to see a message from one of her friends telling her they understood but it wasn't. Kia was far from disappointed however when she saw the name Xander on the screen. Her friend's may have abandoned her but there was still someone in Kia's life that had the instant ability to make her feel on top of the world again.

Chapter Twelve

Kia shivered, pulling her jacket tighter around her, wishing she had chosen something a little more substantial than the thin blue summer jacket she was wearing. August was rapidly giving way to September and the warm summer weather was leaving with it.

Feeling bored and restless Kia had decided to take a drive to the lake, more to kill time than for any real desire to go there, although she did still get the same enjoyment as ever in driving her beloved black mini as she had from the day she got it. A visit to the lake, however, wasn't half as much fun without Xander by her side. Then again nothing seemed as good any more unless he was involved in it. Although the "L word" had yet to be uttered by either of them Kia had thought it to herself many times.

Sitting on a bench beside the water, Kia casually tossed small pebbles into the lake, mindlessly watching the ripples form before slowly dissipating. It was nowhere near as good as the time Xander had shown off by skipping stones across the water's surface. For the tenth time in as many minutes Kia wished he was by her side.

Why did he have to work anyway?

Kia knew she was being a little petulant, as she had been when she had begged him to call in sick and spend the day with her. Although she felt deeply disappointed that he had refused, Kia couldn't deny that she was also a little proud of Xander that he took his job so seriously and wasn't prepared to let his colleagues or employers down. Just her.

Sighing deeply Kia shook her head and told herself to stop being so childish. She would be seeing him the following night and that would have to be good enough, no matter how much she might miss him in the meantime.

The sound of voices made Kia look up. A group of teenagers were on the other side of the lake laughing and pretending they were about to push each other in. Kia remembered when she used to come to the lake with her friends, in fact they had played that same game. Kia recalled the time Sofia had lost her balance during such horseplay and had ended up waist deep in the cold water, her friends hardly able to pull her out from laughing so hard. Kia missed them terribly. She had lost count of the times she had picked up the phone to call or text only to remember they no longer seemed to want anything to do with her.

Kia was initially relieved that neither Sofia nor Rebekah seemed to have told her secret to anyone, no hordes had come knocking at her door threatening to burn the "witch", but neither had the girls replied to any of her texts or emails. Three weeks had passed since the fateful day when she had revealed herself to them and in that time there had been no contact at all, Kia was starting to lose hope that there ever would be.

Picking up a larger stone Kia threw it at the water with force, enjoying the sound of the splash and the mini torrent of water that rose in its wake before the lake settled back to being glass calm, as if she had done nothing at all.

"Your mum said you would be here."

Kia jumped at the unexpected voice behind her, she had been so engrossed in staring at the water that she hadn't heard anyone approach.

Kia grinned as she turned around on the bench already recognising the voice, she should, she had heard it more than a million times before.

"Sof, what are you doing here? Is Rebs with you?"

"She's just finding somewhere to park... I said I'd come and find you while she did."

"You came here to look for me?" Kia was stunned and elated at the same time. They might have been ignoring her but finally they had made contact. This could only be a good thing. Couldn't it?

"Yeah. I... we thought it was about time." Sofia hovered a few steps away from Kia, not quite able to bring herself to join her friend on the bench. It was Kia, just Kia, and yet somehow it wasn't. That had all changed; she had changed.

"So how've you been?" Kia asked, aware of how awkward they both felt and how banal her small talk sounded. "I've missed you both."

"You dropped a bombshell on us K, you couldn't expect us to just carry on as if everything was the same."

"But it is..."

"No it isn't," Sofia said, interrupting her friend. "Can't you see that? You were one of us, we were all the same and now... now you're not... I don't know what you are."

Kia's eyes began to shine as she blinked back tears, disappointment clawing at her chest as she began to suspect her friends were never going to be able to accept her now.

"Then give me a chance," Kia said quietly, her fingers absentmindedly twisting the silver bangle around her wrist. "At least let me explain it to you... Please Sof, doesn't our friendship deserve that?"

"Here you are." Rebekah said as she approached, her hands on her hips and her breathing a little heavy as if she had ran to find them. Tilting her head as she looked at Kia Rebekah frowned. "You look just the same," she said curiously.

"I am just the same," Kia said, trying to keep the frustration out of her voice and not succeeding entirely. "Please, will you both just sit down, you won't catch anything off me you know!"

Exchanging glances the two friends shrugged and walked slowly to the bench, Kia could almost see them both calculating who would be the one having to end up sitting beside her, shuffling to the end of the bench Kia made it a little easier for them, at least that way neither would end up having to sit close enough to touch her.

"I've missed you both," Kia said, rubbing her hand over her eyes to wipe away the tear that still lingered there.

"You think we haven't missed you too?" Sofia asked, "It's not been the same without you… It's always been the three of us…"

"And there is no reason it shouldn't still be," Kia said, reaching out a hand to touch Sofia but then retracting it when she saw her friend flinch. "Please… can't we get past this?"

"I don't know."

Sudden screams from across the lake drew the three girls' attention, they had been so engrossed in their own conversation that the noises from the other side of the water that had been little more than background sounds before, were now one of the teenage girls screaming hysterically.

"Shit!" Rebekah said as she jumped to her feet, "Someone is in the water …"

Rebekah was already running around the lake before her two friends had got to their feet and by the time they arrived she was helping one of the teenage boys pull his friend from the water.

"We just thought he was mucking about," one of the dark haired boys said, his eyes filled with tears as he looked down at the prostrate form of his friend. "I mean he's a good swimmer so when he didn't come back up from under the water right away... we though he was just showing off."

"It looks like he cracked his head on something," Rebekah said, brushing the unconscious boy's hair back to reveal a wound on his forehead.

"Is he breathing?" A blonde haired girl asked, she was dancing nervously from one foot to the other and biting at her fingers. "It doesn't look like he's breathing!"

"I don't think he is," Rebekah said, her eyes fixed on Kia.

"Someone has to give him that CPR thing," Another of the teenage girls said, her tone equally as hysterical as her friends.

"Has anyone called an ambulance?" Kia asked, her tone calm and authoritative. The teenagers all looked at each other and shook their heads. "Then somebody do that. Now!"

Kia knelt down at the boys side facing Rebekah, their eyes locked for a few seconds.

"He's dead," Rebekah mouthed so that only Kia could see.

"I can help him," Kia said quietly, her voice barely a whisper.

"Do it!"

Leaning over the boy so that no one could see Kia placed her hands on his chest and closed her eyes. Her hand instantly began to burn, a sensation that ran the length of her arm causing her pulse to race for a second as the glow of light radiated from her palm.

After a moment the boy began to cough, Kia and Rebekah turned him onto his side to let him cough the water from his lungs.

"Did you give him CPR?" One of the teenagers asked in awe.

"Yeah," Kia said getting to her feet and rubbing at the leftover tingling in her palm. "Yeah I did."

"Oh thank you, thank you," The nervous blonde girl said, launching herself at Kia and embracing her fiercely. "I don't know what I would have done if you hadn't saved him."

"That's okay," Kia said as she disentangled herself from the girl, relieved to hear the sound of the ambulance drawing close, and began to walk away.

"You're not sticking around?" The girl asked. "You're like a hero or something..."

"No," Rebekah said running a few steps to catch up with Kia and taking her friend's hand. "We've got somewhere to be."

"Yeah," Sofia agreed, her fingers lacing with Kia's on the other side. "The paramedics will look after your friend now."

Kia smiled, her heart ready to burst as she walked hand in hand with her two dearest friends.

"It's time we looked after ours," Sofia said quietly.

"That was amazing," Rebekah said somewhat in awe. "I mean... that kid could have died... like actually died... If you hadn't..."

"So not so scary any more?" Kia asked.

"Are you joking?" Sofia said with a half laugh. "We just saw you bring someone back to life, it doesn't get much scarier than that!"

"Oh..."

"Scary... but amazing..."

"But mostly amazing," Rebekah said, squeezing Kia's hand tightly, "I'm sorry about how I acted before K."

"That's okay."

"No it's not, we're your mates and we should have been there for you... it was just... you know."

"Yeah I know."

"So?" Sofia said, stopping and turning to face Kia. "What exactly happened... how are you suddenly like this?"

"It's a long story," Kia said.

"We're in no rush."

"Okay... so like a long time ago... I mean a long, long time ago there was this Goddess called Assaie..."

Chapter Thirteen

"When are you bringing him home?"

"Mum!"

"I mean it Kia, you've been seeing this young man for over a month now and I've yet to meet him."

"I just don't want to jinx things," Kia said with a shrug. She knew that her mother was right and if it had been any other boy she would have had no hesitation in bringing him home for the obligatory introductions, but Xander was different, special, and Kia was scared of upsetting the status quo and ruining things. What if he thought she was getting too heavy wanting to do the "meet the parents" thing and he backed off?

"Well just ask him to pick you up from home for once, let me at least get a look at him."

"I dunno."

"Come on Kia, I just want to see the boy that obviously means so much to you. I'll answer the door to him, say "hello" and that'll be it. Promise."

"Promise?"

"I said so didn't I?"

"Well... okay I suppose..." Kia shrugged, she knew she was being a little unreasonable. After all she had already met both of Xander's parents, although that was because they were working in the restaurant one night when she and Xander were having a meal. They had always been out on the few occasions Xander had taken her back home. "But just a "hello" ... no cross examining him over his intentions or anything!"

"As if I would!" Katherine said, tossing her hair back as if mightily offended at the suggestion.

***

Kia felt sick. Her stomach had begun to churn as she got dressed and now, as she applied the finishing touches to her make up, it was practically doing somersaults. At any moment Xander would ring the doorbell and her mother would answer. What if they didn't like each other? What if her mother thought Xander wasn't good enough for her daughter. What if her mother thought Xander was perfect for her daughter and started hinting at engagements and weddings. Kia's queasiness went up a notch.

Then the doorbell rang.

"You must be Xander," Katherine said with a smile as she opened the door. She could certainly see what her daughter saw in this young man, he was even more handsome up close compared to the glimpse she had caught of him a few weeks earlier when she had dropped Kia off for their first date.

"Mrs. Deering," Xander said with a bright smile that made his eyes look more blue than grey. "I can see where Kia gets her good looks.

"Call me Katherine," Katherine said with a smile, finding herself charmed despite his cheesy line, "Kia said you were a bit of a charmer." Katherine stepped back to allow Xander inside. "She'll be down in a second."

"It's not charm when it's true Mrs... Katherine."

"I can see I'll have to keep an eye on you. So, Kia tells me you're a mechanic?"

"Yeah that's right, I had a look at the mini you got Kia for her birthday, it's a good little runner, you made a good choice there."

"Shame we didn't know you then I could have got you to give it the once over."

"Well any time it needs looking at I've already told Kee to let me know."

"Xander, hi," Kia said, breathless as she raced down the stairs. "Are we ready to go then?"

"Ready when you are... wow you look gorgeous."

"Xand!" Kia blushed deeply. No matter how many times Xander complimented her it still made her redden but that wasn't to say she didn't enjoy it all the same.

"He's not wrong sweetheart," Katherine said kissing her daughter's cheek. "You two have a nice night."

"Pleasure to meet you Katherine," Xander said holding out his hand.

"You too," Katherine said reaching out her own hand to his.

The second their hands touched Katherine's expression changed from one of charmed delight to cold horror.

"Oh no..no..no..." Katherine said dropping Xander's hand as if it burned and stumbling backwards. "Please no..."

"Mum what is it?" Kia said, racing to her mother's side, her face heavy with concern.

"Do you not know what he is?"

"What he... what do you mean?"

"How could you bring him into our house?"

"Mum what are you talking about? I don't understand..."

"Katherine... Mrs. Deering?" Xander stepped towards her, stopping when he saw the look of fear on her face grow. "What do you think I have done?"

"It's not what you've done it's what you... what you are... who you are..."

"My name's Xander Matthews and I am a mechanic."

"I know what you are," Katherine said, her initial shock passing Katherine stepped back towards him and stared deep into his eyes, her own eyes dark with accusation. "You're a son of Isydro!"

"Mum you don't know what you're... he can't be..." Kia tried to find the words to argue with her mother's declaration but she already knew it must be the truth, a few seconds of silence had passed and Xander had neither asked who Isydro was or denied any knowledge of him. "Xand?"

"How do you know of Isydro?" Xander asked, the only other person he had ever heard mention that name was his own father and yet here was his girlfriend's mother talking of the God as if the name were common knowledge.

"Why? Did you think you could hide your terrible secret from us?" Katherine asked, her lips curled in disgust.

"I have no terrible secret," Xander said calmly as the realisation of the situation began to dawn on him. "But you obviously know of my ancestor and that can only mean..."

"Yes." Katherine said firmly, her jaw tightly clenched. "We are the descendants of the Goddess your ancestor murdered and now here you are and you expect me to welcome Isydro's heir into my home?"

"No mum," Kia said, taking a deep breath as she stepped between her mother and boyfriend. "I am asking you to welcome my boyfriend into our home. Xander is not Isydro any more than we are Assaie."

"But you know what Isydro did, you think we should just forget that?"

"What Isydro did, not Xander… and do you not remember what Assaie told Jacob? It's not that long ago you told me the story mum, she asked him not to blame the Gods, not to hate them."

"That doesn't mean I want my daughter anywhere near one of their children."

"Mrs. Deering," Xander said, his hands taking Kia's shoulders gently but firmly as he moved her slightly to one side. "I'm sorry I hadn't told Kia who I am, how was I to know it was something she would understand, she never mentioned the Goddess to me either."

"That's hardly the same thing," Katherine said with a sneer. "Our ancestor wasn't a cold blooded killer."

"And neither was mine." Xander had to concentrate hard to keep his breathing calm and his voice level, the last thing he wanted to do was to raise his voice in front of a woman who already had such a low opinion of him. "I'm sure the story of Assaie's life on earth has been passed down through the generations, well so has Isydro's… but I doubt you have heard the rest of his story… before you condemn him, and me, at least give me the chance to argue his case."

"Mum please," Kia said softly, not realising that she had taken Xander's hand as he spoke.

"Why should I?"

"Because I'm in love with your daughter." Xander's words came out so matter of fact, as if it was something that had been discussed between the couple already, and they made Kia's heart sing with joy despite the less than perfect way in which he had let her know how he felt.

"You are?" Kia asked, her eyes nearly as wide as her smile.

"I thought you knew."

"You know I love you too don't you?"

"Yeah I know." Xander squeezed Kia's hand tightly before they both turned their attention back to Katherine. "Well?" Xander asked her. "Do I get a chance?"

Looking between her daughter and the man she obviously cared deeply for Katherine felt her resolve begin to crumble as her anger faded. Her empathy often needed direct physical contact with the other person for Katherine to truly feel what they felt, but the love emanating off the couple before her could more than likely be felt even by someone not so gifted.

"We'd better go and sit down," Katherine said as she turned and headed back towards the living room, seating herself on the single chair, her back straight as if to attention and her hands on her lap laced so tightly together that her knuckles were beginning to whiten. In all the years since she had learned of Assaie she hadn't really given Isydro more than a fleeting thought but when suddenly and unexpectedly faced with one of his descendants Katherine had been surprised by the strength of her anger, and her fear for Kia.

Xander took a seat on the sofa beside Kia, their hands still locked together although his attention was focussed on Katherine as he began to speak.

***

Isydro ran from Assaie's small house, neither noticing nor caring about the strange looks he attracted or the sounds of anger when he knocked into someone, he just had to get away. As far away as he could from the terrible thing he had done.

He ran until his feet were raw and his lungs battled for air, his skin stung from the combination of wind and the heat from the sun which shone down from a cloudless blue sky.

Finally, when Isydro had no more energy to go any further he stumbled to a stop, collapsing in a heap by a large water butt on the outskirts of a village a few miles from the one where Assaie lived, where Assaie had lived. There was little doubt she would have died of her wounds and that he had killed her.

Curling himself up into a ball Isydro howled. Never before, as either God or human, had he experienced such grief or such guilt and the feelings both shocked and terrified him.

If this was being human then he didn't want it, he wanted to return back to the heavens, back where he belonged.

"Are you okay mister?"

Isydro looked up toward the young voice that addressed him. The girl looked young, perhaps as little as six or seven years old and yet she looked at him unflinchingly, despite his ragged and wild appearance.

"Are you hurt?" The girl asked, tilting her head to get a better look at him. "I heard you crying."

"I'm not hurt," Isydro said, shuffling into a sitting position and trying to force a smile onto his face.

"You have blood on you."

Isydro looked down and his tunic and felt sickened. "I'm not hurt," he repeated.

"Are you lost then? I cried once when I was lost, but that was when I was young..."

"You're still young."

The girl shrugged as if his words didn't make much sense. Dragging her hands through her dirty blonde hair she bent down to pick up the wooden bucket she had placed down when she stopped to speak to him. Her dress looked as if it had been fashioned from an old piece of sack but for a frame much larger than hers, a strand of rope was tied around her middle and her feet were dirty and bare.

"What are you doing out here on your own?" Isydro asked, getting to his feet and watching as she lifted her bucket into the water butt, laying it on its side in the water to let it fill slowly.

"Getting water silly."

"Where's your papa?"

The girl shrugged. "I don't have one."

"Where's your mama then?"

"She's back at home."

"And she sent you out for the water."

"I'm a big girl now," the girl said, obviously struggling to lift the now filled and heavy bucket out of the butt. "Mama says I have to help out with the chores... she can't do these things no more."

"Why can't she?"

"Mama got awful sick and now she stays in her bed."

"So who looks after you?"

The girl frowned as if she had never considered that question before. "I do," she said finally, "I have to go... mama is waiting for me." Gritting her teeth the girl lifted the bucket of water with both hands, holding it between her legs as she began to stagger back into the village.

Scooping some water from the butt into his hands Isydro splashed his face, running his hands back into his hair, smoothing down some of the wildness, before he jogged after the girl.

"How about you let me carry that for you?" Isydro said, holding out one hand.

"Why?"

"Because I want to help you."

The girl stopped and put the bucket down on the ground before turning to face the strange man.

"Why?" She asked again.

"I don't know... to be nice... don't other people offer to help you to be nice?"

"No," the girl said in a matter of fact tone. "People don't normally talk to us... I don't think they like mama very much."

"Why not?"

"No one ever told me... she said it doesn't matter what other people think because she has me."

"Well she is very lucky that she does," Isydro said as he picked up the water bucket. "What's your name?"

"Daisie."

"That's a pretty name." Isydro said. "It's nice to meet you Daisie, I'm..." Isydro paused. He no longer wanted to use the name of William, it felt tarnished; William was the name of the man who had killed the woman Phae.

"Do you not know your own name?" Daisie asked with a giggle that reminded Isydro just how young the girl was.

"I seem to have forgotten it," Isydro said with a laugh.

Daisie giggled some more as she began to skip ahead. "I'll call you Henry," She called back over her shoulder.

"Why Henry?" Isydro asked as he set off after her.

"I have to call you something."

Isydro smiled, he couldn't fault the child's logic.

As they walked into the village Isydro noticed the dark looks thrown in Daisie's direction but the child seemed oblivious as she skipped along and it saddened Isydro that such treatment was obviously so common to her that she no longer even noticed.

"This way Henry," Daisie called cheerfully. "Mama will be pleased that so much water made it home without me spilling it."

Daisie stopped outside a run down wooden building, more of a shack than a house, the door hung at an uneven angle and it appeared that the bottom hinge had rusted through and snapped. With both hands on the large metal handle Daisie pulled the door open and stepped inside.

"You'll have to keep quiet," Daisie whispered as Isydro followed her inside. "Mama is still sleeping, and she doesn't like me to wake her when she sleeps. I'll set the stew cooking over the fire, the smell of that usually wakes her."

Looking around the small shack Isydro couldn't help but shudder. It was clear that Daisie had been left in sole charge of the home for some time.

Every surface was dirty, the hard stone floor was caked with dried mud and, when Isydro spotted the bed in the corner of the single room it was obvious the bed linen had not been washed for a very long time.

Isydro hardly noticed the woman lying in the bed at first, she was so thin and frail, her dirty hair covering half of her face making her blend in with the unwashed bedding.

Taking a step forward Isydro stopped, it wasn't just a dirty house he smelt.

"Daisie when did mama last wake up?"

"Not for a couple of days... but she doesn't like me to wake her."

Moving closer to the bed Isydro reached out a hand and touched it to the cheek of its occupant, she was ice cold, Isydro knew that she would never be waking again.

"Daisie," Isydro said kindly as he sat down on the three-legged wooden stool that was beside the open fireplace and beckoned the girl towards him.

"Yes Henry?"

"Daisie do you know what dead is?"

"Of course I do... we had a goat once, she gave us nice milk, but then mama told me the goat couldn't give us milk no more so she had to be made dead... we had nice stew for lots of days after that."

"I'm sorry Daisie but I'm afraid your mama is dead."

"But she's asleep."

"No Daisie... mama won't wake up again."

Daisie looked from Isydro to her mother and back again, recognition of his words slowly sinking in.

"Mama's with the Goddesses now?"

"I think she is, yes."

"Oh." Slumping down onto the floor silent tears rolled down Daisie's cheeks. "Mama was all I had..." she sobbed, her tears leaving trails in the dirt on her cheeks. "Who will care for me now?"

"I will Daisie," Isydro said, pulling the weeping child onto his lap and rocking her as she wept. "I'll look after you from now on... everything will be all right now Daisie. I promise."

Holding Daisie tightly Isydro closed his eyes. In another village he knew that a little girl now had to grow up without her mother, there was nothing he could do to change that and he would never forgive himself for being the cause of it, but he silently vowed that he would do all he could to give Daisie the life she deserved.

***

"And did he?" Katherine asked once Xander had finished talking.

"He did," Xander said, "He took her away from that village and from that day they were known as father and daughter... Isydro made sure she never went without again, and that she got to be the child she was meant to be."

"So where did Isydro's line come from?" Kia asked, brushing away a few tears from her cheeks that she hadn't been aware of shedding as Xander had told Isydro's tale.

***

Isydro was getting worried, Daisie had taken too long getting bread from the market, it wasn't far and it was a journey she had made countless times in the three years they had lived in the village. He was just considering going to look for her when there was a knock at the door of their small house. It was a similar building to the one Daisie had grown up in but Isydro ensured that it was always clean and warm; his adopted daughter was never going to suffer needlessly again.

When he opened the door he was greeted by the smile of a blonde woman, her green eyes were kind as she looked at him and it took him a few seconds to realise she was holding onto Daisie's hand.

"I believe this young lady belongs to you," the woman said when Isydro failed to speak.

"Yes, yes, sorry, thank you," Isydro stuttered, surprised to find himself feeling flustered under her gaze.

"I found her in the market, she said she couldn't remember her way home."

"Daisie?" Isydro said in a mildly accusing tone. "You've been to the market thousands of times... why did you tell this nice lady you didn't know your way home."

Daisie grinned as she skipped into the house.

"Papa gets lonely," she said in matter of fact way as she placed the bread on the table. "I thought he should have a friend." Turning to Isydro she smiled broadly. "She's pretty Henry, you should invite her in."

"I am so sorry," Isydro said.

"Don't be, she is quite adorable, your wife must be very proud."

Isydro hesitated before wording a reply that was neither a lie nor the complete truth. "Daisie's mother died a few years ago."

"I am sorry to hear that."

"Can I offer you a drink, to thank you for bringing my wayward child home?"

"Yes, thank you… that would be most welcome."

***

"Not long after Daisie brought Clara home Isydro asked her to marry him," Xander said, "She adored Daisie and treated her as her own child, even after they were blessed with a son Daisie was never neglected, Isydro made sure of it… he couldn't make up to Althaia for what he had done but he made sure another motherless child didn't have to suffer."

"Isydro did all that?" Katherine said, her voice slightly hushed and her brow furrowed with uncertainty.

"He wasn't a monster," Xander said with a warm smile. "In fact at the time he was just a man, a man who made a terrible mistake. Maybe he was wrong in running off like he did and leaving Assaie, but if he hadn't …"

"He probably wouldn't have met Daisie," Katherine said, finishing Xander's thought. "And who knows what might have happened to that poor little girl then… at least Althaia always had Jacob to care for her."

Getting to her feet Katherine rubbed at her eyes, she felt suddenly quite exhausted, the emotional upset of the past hour having taken its toll, Her gift meant that she felt such things more keenly than other people might, just like she could feel the truth in Xander's words, and such strong emotions could be terribly draining. Despite her initial reaction Katherine knew the truth in not just her own heart but also in the hearts of the two young people before her, Assaie didn't blame Isydro for her death so who was she to second guess a Goddess?

"Weren't you two going out?" Katherine said with a tired smile.

"You don't mind?" Kia asked, getting to her feet and taking her mother's hand.

"It was just a shock," Katherine said, "Feeling the power of Isydro's line when I touched Xander's hand." Turning to Xander Katherine smiled. "But I shouldn't have reacted the way that I did and I apologise. My daughter is obviously very fond of you... and who am I to question that?"

"There's nothing for you to apologise for," Xander said graciously, also rising to his feet to stand behind Kia, one hand resting lightly on her shoulder as if he we drawn to touch her without even realising. "You were just looking out for Kia... and I can understand that... I would do whatever I could to protect her as well."

"You know, I believe you would." Katherine couldn't believe how differently she felt in such a short space of time but she was never one to avoid admitting when she was wrong, and she'd been wrong about Xander. Kia would be safe with him, Katherine knew that now, safe and protected. "Now go on with the pair of you, get out and enjoy yourselves, I'm ready for a little peace and quiet."

"She means she's ready to doze off in front of the TV," Kia teased, pecking a kiss to her mother's cheek before giving her a quick hug.

"See what a child I raised?" Katherine said, raising her eyes to the ceiling in horror, the smile on her face revealing her true feelings. "I bet you never speak to your mother like that do you Xander."

Xander couldn't help but laugh, the warm friendly banter between mother and daughter was a pleasure to witness and so far from his own relationship with his far more formal parents. "Well maybe a little," Xander said, "But even so... Kia is lucky to have you."

"Right that's it," Kia said, grabbing hold of Xander's hand and dragging him, somewhat overdramatically towards the door. "We're going before my mother decides to adopt you... because that would just be weird!"

Katherine stood at the window for a long time after Kia and Xander had disappeared out of sight. Her mind filled with thoughts of the Gods and

Goddesses who once watched over the world and the people in it, how strange it was that they were now all but forgotten. Looking up to the clear night sky Katherine marvelled at the brilliance of the almost full moon and scattering of diamond stars and she wondered if Assaie was even up in the heavens any more watching over her line.

"I hope you're proud of us," Katherine whispered into the night, somehow feeling that her words were heard.

Stifling a yawn, she returned to the chair, reached for the remote control, turned on the television and settled down to watch a gentle comedy, before promptly falling fast asleep.

Chapter Fourteen

Kia and Xander hadn't planned to return to the park where they had ended their first date, and shared their first kiss, but then none of the evening had panned out the way they had imagined.

After leaving Kia's house neither of them felt in the mood for the planned cinema trip and instead they found themselves walking hand in hand under the glow of a bright moon discussing the strange revelations of the evening.

"So when did you know... about Isydro and everything?" Kia asked as she sat down on the bench that held very happy memories.

"My father told me when I turned eighteen," Xander said, sitting beside her, his arm instinctively going around her shoulders to pull her closer to him.

"Same for me," Kia said, snuggling in to rest her head on Xander's shoulder. "Did you think he was crazy or something?"

"No, not really."

"I thought mum had gone mental, or was just making it up!"

"My father isn't really one for stories, if he tells you something you can generally guarantee it's a fact."

"Even so, it's one hell of a fact!"

"What do you think the chances are Kia?"

"Of what?"

"The two of us... meeting... and... you know."

Sitting up again, Kia turned to look into Xander's eyes. "I dunno, maybe it was just meant to be."

He looked so handsome, so very perfect that Kia couldn't imagine a single thing she would ever want to change about him, and then without warning she began to laugh. "I can't believe the first time you say you love me and it's to my mother!"

"It was kind of an important moment!"

"Saying that always is..."

"No, I meant..."

"I know... I was teasing."

"Kia?"

"Yeah."

Xander took hold of Kia's hands tightly. He knew that she had no idea of her true beauty and that only served to make her even more so. "Kia Deering... I do love you... so much."

With a bright smile that almost rivalled the glow of the moon Kia leant forward and kissed Xander's soft lips tenderly, her body moving instinctively towards his as their kiss intensified until it was all they could do to contain themselves in such a relatively public place.

"Xand?" Kia said slightly breathlessly.

"Yeah?"

"You know how I said your room was a dump and I would never set foot in it again without it being sanitised?"

"Yeah..."

"I may have been a little hasty..."

"Are you propositioning me Miss Deering?"

"And are you objecting Mr. Matthews?"

Jumping to his feet Xander reached out his hands and pulled Kia up after him, automatically propelling her into his arms for another heated kiss.

"Not for a second," he said when they finally pulled apart again. "But just so you know, I cleaned up this morning."

"I hope you weren't presuming..."

"Well I knew you couldn't resist me for long..."

"I could still change my mind."

Stroking Kia's cheek with one finger Xander smiled gently, his eyes sparkling with the love he had so recently professed. "But you won't!"

***

"I should be getting home," Kia said, stretching in the warm comfort of Xander's bed and not actually making any effort to get up.

"You could always stay," Xander said, turning his head to kiss her bare shoulder.

"Mum might worry."

"Call her..."

"I dunno..." Kia felt torn. Part of her wanted nothing more than to stay where she was and fall to sleep in the warmth and safety of Xander's arms, but another part of her didn't like the idea of leaving Katherine alone in the house all night. "No I should go... besides your folks will be home soon and I don't want them to find me here...like this," she said finally, sitting up right and shivering as the cool air touched her skin.

Xander ran a finger down the length of Kia's back, thinking of a hundred different ways of talking her into staying but instead all he said was "Okay, if you really want to."

"It's not that I don't want to stay, I just..."

"It's okay, really... another time."

Pulling on her clothes Kia ran a hand through her hair and was surprised at how tangled it felt.

"I must look a fright," she said.

"You look lovely," Xander insisted, unable to resist pulling her back onto the bed for another languorous kiss. "You always do."

"Xand stop it," Kia objected, her smiles and laughs conflicting with her words. "I'll never leave at this rate!"

"Wouldn't that be a shame," Xander said with a grin, but he still got off the bed and allowed her to finish dressing.

In no real rush to leave Xander's side Kia was happy to accept his offer to walk her home, although it was almost midnight and a taxi would have been a more sensible option, both of them knew that they just wanted to prolong the time they had together.

The streets were quiet and hardly a car passed them as they walked hand in hand in comfortable silence, enjoying the simple act of being in each other's presence underneath the bright shining stars.

"Xand?" Kia said after a while, her thoughts having been focussed on their shared and unexpected lineage.

"Yeah?"

"Did Isydro leave anything for his sons?"

"Leave anything?"

"Yeah... you know... like a gift?"

"Gift?"

Kia paused, perhaps the special gifts that Assaie had bequeathed were not something Isydro had also done and she felt unsure if she should carry on.

"Doesn't matter."

"No, tell me what you mean."

"I just thought, maybe... like some kind of ability... but no, forget it..."

Xander closed his eyes for a second, his fist clenched tightly, when both were opened he held out his hand, palm up, to Kia. The skin of his palm was marked, almost as if it had been branded, by the image of a circle intersected by a single line. The look of the mark was so familiar that Kia held up her own hand, the image of the Goddess pendant quickly becoming visible.

Without discussion they pressed their palms together, the connection of the marks creating a heat that almost felt painful and yet not something either of them felt a desire to break away from.

Their eyes locked as they stood for countless minutes, motionless and silent, yet communicating in a way neither had ever known possible. The depths of each other's hearts and minds opened up as easily as a book, the stories of their lives there for the other to read and understand.

The connection was so intense that when they finally let go of each other's hand they both staggered backwards, dazed and stunned.

"You can heal?" Xander said in awe, tilting his head as he looked at the girl who was so much more than just a girl. "That's just... wow..."

"Yeah, yeah it's taken some getting used to," Kia said, her body trembling slightly in aftershock, she could still feel the connection to Xander even though they were no longer touching. "And you..."

Xander let his eyes look up to the dark heavens, Kia mirroring his gaze. Suddenly the twinkling shiny stars seemed to multiply with growing ferocity, tumbling downwards in such a matter that Kia closed her eyes shut in a knee jerk reaction. It was only when she felt the familiar damp sensation against her skin did she open them.

'Snow?'

"I know! Healing is so much cooler. But I can also do this." Within seconds the midnight sky was beginning to glow with a sunrise of such intense hues of red, orange and yellow and Kia couldn't help but giggle at the clap of thunder and the sudden heavy rain.

'Can you make it summer again?' Kia asked, with deadpan sincerity. Not only were the changes in the weather a little unnerving but it could well draw some unwanted attention should it go on for too long.

"As you command," Xander said with an over the top flourish, arcing his arms over his head and the night returned to its nondescript former state.

Shaking the rain from her hair Kia looked up into the sky, now so calm and still, it was hard to believe that only seconds earlier it had been stormy.

"That was quite a show," she said with a smile, shivering a little at the lingering cold on her skin.

"I aim to please," Xander said. "But you though, I mean, how does this healing thing even work?"

"Well... you know..."

"Not really. That's why I asked... manipulating the weather a bit is one thing... but healing, I can't even imagine. How does it... what do you... I mean what do you actually DO?"

Kia laughed. "Well it's not easy to explain, I could show you though, if you had a knife."

"What? You want to stab me?"

"Well I could... but a cut usually suffices."

"You know what," Xander said with a smile that also wrinkled his brow, "I think I might pass."

"Don't you trust me?"

"Of course I do," Xander said grabbing a hold of Kia's hand firmly, his smile brightening as he looked into her eyes. For a moment he had been afraid that her words were serious but her cheeky grin and the dancing laughter in her eyes assured Xander that Kia was teasing him.

With an exaggerated sigh Kia pulled away from Xander's hand, swinging her arms as she skipped a few steps ahead of him.

"Poor me," Kia said with another sigh, "What kind of boyfriend do I have that won't let me cut him up a little bit?"

"A sensible one," Xander said, catching up with Kia and slipping his arm around her middle, pulling her close beside him as he brushed a soft kiss against her lips. "Seriously though K," he said, stepping back and tilting his head to one side as he observed the young woman who he had a feeling would always be a source of constant amazement and joy. "How does it feel? What do you... what CAN you do?"

Kia thought for a moment before replying. "It's like this rush of... I don't know, power or energy or something. I can feel it pouring from my hands, and it burns but at the same time it feels like... Life!"

"Sounds kinda exhausting."

"Yeah, it can be... but it's a good exhausting."

"So what sort of things can you heal?"

"I'm not completely sure, I think there are limits though... like I couldn't just cure someone of cancer or whatever... It's like some things are natural and are meant to happen... people have to die after all."

"Die? You don't mean you can actually "heal" the dead?"

"Well... erm..."

"You can't... can you?"

"Well, yeah... I mean I think so... that is I think I have..."

"Wow," Xander took a deep breath, he hadn't realised the true extent of Kia's abilities. "My little weather show seems pretty lame in comparison to that."

"Not at all," Kia said, nudging Xander playfully before pulling his arm around her shoulders. "Besides when I'm cold in the middle of winter I know where to come when I fancy a summers day."

"I don't know about a day... I can maybe do you half an hour... that's pretty exhausting too you know."

"Ah well in that case you'll just have to find other ways to keep me warm the rest of the time."

As one Kia and Xander began to walk again, slowly making their way back to Kia's home, neither of them noticing how brightly the moon was shining in the midnight black sky, it was nowhere near as enthralling as the things they could see in each other.

*

It was well past midnight by the time Xander got back home, the goodbye he had shared with Kia had been long and reluctant and his feet unwilling to take each step that had moved him further from her side. He had never known such intensity of feelings as those he had for Kia and they both exhilarated and terrified him in equal measure. Her presence in Xander's life made him feel that anything was possible, and the idea that she may ever part from him was an impossibility that could never be entertained.

As he approached the two storey detached house that he shared with his parents Xander saw that the downstairs lights were glowing, a sign that his mother and father were sharing a late night glass of wine after a long shift at the restaurant.

"Is that you sweetheart?" Suzanna's voice called from the kitchen as Xander pushed open the front door. "We're through here."

"Hi," Xander said as he entered the kitchen, leaning against the doorframe he regarded his parents with a smile. Although they couldn't ever claim to have never had a cross word, indeed some of their fights had been enough to make the windows rattle, their marriage was as solid and loving as it had been on the day they exchanged vows. With a smile, Xander made a silent wish that he too would be as content in marriage, a thought that caught him by surprise as marriage had always been so very far from his thoughts.

"All right son?" George asked, tilting his head slightly as he observed his son, he couldn't remember ever seeing such a contemplative look on the young man's face before.

"Yeah I... I've just taken Kia home," Xander said, scraping back a chair and sitting beside his mother at the small table, resting his elbows on the polished wooden surface and cupping his chin with his hands.

"Such a pretty girl," George said with a wink, which earned him a dig in the ribs from his wife.

"Yeah she's... she's great," Xander agreed, chewing against the inside of his cheek.

"What's wrong love?" Suzanna said, displaying her usual insightfulness as she patted her son's arm.

"I dunno it's just..." Xander stopped, unsure if he should say more, if it even mattered. He felt a little light-headed as if he were inside a snow globe and someone had shaken it up. "You know how," Xander began, his voice wavering a little with uncertainty, "Like... you know... you think you know where your life's going and it's all pretty sorted and then ... and then things change... something changes in a way you don't expect and..."

Suzanna's grip on her son's arm tightened suddenly as she let out a small gasp of fright, her motherly instincts instantly jumping to the worst possible conclusion. "Are you sick? Is it serious? Oh sweetheart what is it?"

"Mum, no, no," Xander said with a small laugh, patting his mother's delicate hand and smiling both amused at and grateful for her worry. "It's nothing like that... you couldn't be further from the truth... in fact it... it's not actually me... not as such... It's about Kia..."

"Oh Xander," George said with slow shake of his head, "You've not gone and got that poor girl in trouble have you?"

"Dad! What do you take me for?"

"A red blooded young man... and I'm not too old to remember what that's like..."

"Well it's not that," Xander said, quickly interrupting his father before he could elaborate further.

"So?" Suzanna said. "We know what it isn't... so how about telling us what this big life changing event is?"

"I... I met K's mum today... and she's really nice... you'd like her... only ..."

"Only?" Suzanna prompted.

"Only when she touched me she knew... what I am," Xander turned to look at his father, "What we are."

"She knew what?" George asked making Xander raise his eyebrows in a familiar 'Dad really' expression. George's eyes widened as realisation hit him. "You mean..?"

"Yeah, she felt Isydro in me."

"But how," George asked, his fingers twisting around the stem of his empty wine glass. "How could she... I mean did you say something... or.. or..."

"Of course I didn't say anything, like I said she felt it..."

"But there's no way... the only ones who could possibly..." George stopped, there was only one explanation but surely that was impossible. "You don't mean?"

"Yeah..."

"What?" Suzanna asked, not quite following the conversation. Despite knowing the full history of her husband's lineage sometimes their apparent short-handed conversations made her feeling left out.

"She's of Assaie's line," Xander explained.

"The Goddess?"

"Exactly."

"Wow, that's…" Suzanna looked at her husband and son in turn, "What does that mean?"

"I don't know," George said, his brow wrinkled in thought, "It's never happened before… no one was even sure that Assaie's line had continued beyond her first child. We never knew what happened after… after Assaie's death… How did Kia's mother react?"

"She freaked out at first," Xander said, "All they knew of Isydro was that he was a killer… they never heard of what he did later to make amends …"

George nodded slowly, it was hard to comprehend. For generations the two lines had existed virtually unaware of each other's presence and now they had come together again, it couldn't just be an accident.

"Are you serious about this girl Xander," George asked sternly.

"Yeah I really… like her," Xander's face flushed slightly, he wanted to say love but felt suddenly shy and embarrassed.

"Then good," George said, refilling his wine glass and taking a large drink. "I think this was meant to be."

Chapter Fifteen

Kia was bored and restless, there were only a couple of days left before college began again and the weather had decided that winter could come early, with gale force winds lashing the torrential rain against her bedroom window as she looked out feeling dejected. If Xander was there he could at least give her the sunshine again for a few minutes but he was working.

It was a little unnerving when Kia realised just how much she had become reliant on Xander's presence, nothing felt quite right when he wasn't around. It was as if he was some kind of exquisite drug and Kia, a more than willing addict. Having someone in her life who got her so completely and loved her so intensely was something Kia had never even dreamed of, it was the sort of thing that only happened in stories, not to real people in their real lives, but then again only a few months ago she would have said Goddesses only existed in stories too.

How much her life had changed. How much better it had become.

With a deep breath Kia swung her legs off the bed and moved away from the window. What was she doing moping about when her life was so amazing? So Xander wasn't around at the moment and the weather was abysmal, that didn't mean she shouldn't be enjoying her last days of freedom did it?

"Mum," Kia shouted as she slipped on her coat and reached for her car keys. "Mum I'm going out."

"Okay sweetheart," Katherine called back from the kitchen where she was busy dicing vegetables. Xander had recently brought her a sack of the most amazingly fresh and delicious vegetables she had ever tried. When she asked where they were from he had replied with a deliberate wink saying his father had a very special way of growing them. "Be careful in this weather."

"I always am." Kia said, her fingers dancing over her mobile phone's keypad asking Sofia and Rebekah to meet her for a drink and a catch up.

The bar was busy when Kia arrived and it took her a few minutes for her to spot Rebekah and Sofia at a side table, a glass of orange juice already waiting for her.

As she approached her friends got to their feet and the three of them embraced.

"So," Sofia said as they all sat down. "Me and Rebs were just discussing what hats we should get?"

"Hats?" Kia asked, her brow furrowed with non-comprehension.

"Yeah you know," Rebekah said with a mischievous twinkle in her eyes and a teasing giggle in her voice. "For attending your wedding... oh, unless you're going to ask us to be bridesmaids?"

"Oh yes please," Sofia joined in, nodding her head vigorously, "Please let us be your bridesmaids K."

"You two are mean," Kia said, smiling despite herself.

"It's not us two that have been MIA lately," Sofia said.

"I know," Kia said, her smile fading slightly. "I know I've been a rubbish mate... I've always hated those girls who dump their friends the second a bloke comes along... but..." With a shrug Kia looked down into her drink. She just couldn't find the words to explain what he meant to her.

"Ah we're only teasing," Rebekah said, reaching across the small table and squeezing Kia's hand. "You're not a rubbish mate... we're happy for you, honest... I mean you could have at least found a bloke with a couple of hot brothers or something, but still."

The easy banter of a long standing friendship continued and Kia was glad she had reconnected with the two girls, vowing she would never leave it so long again without seeing them.

After a few hours the bar began to empty, Kia had just about had her fill of fruit juice and Rebekah was starting to show the effects of the vodkas she had been drinking.

"Anyone want a lift home?" Kia asked as she got to her feet.

"Yeah please," Sofia said.

"Oh well if we're going," Rebekah answered, her tone making it clear she would have gladly stayed until closing time given the chance.

"Come on you," Kia said hoisting Rebekah to her feet and guiding her towards the pub door.

The screaming was the first thing Kia heard as the pub door swung open followed by a screech of breaks and then the sickening crunch of metal that echoed a sound she had heard once before. There was no mistaking the sound of a collision between two vehicles as metal grated against metal, glass shattered and then the continuous tone of a car horn.

Instinct kicked in and Kia handed Rebekah over to Sofia's keeping before she ran to the crossroads where the collision had taken place, of all the people gathering around the site Kia knew that she could be the most useful.

Most of the gathered crowd were simply standing in the downpour watching the drama unfold before them, while a few pulled at car doors, shouting to drivers and passengers asking if they were all right.

Kia recognised the sight of a teenage boy stretched out on the floor, his body stained with blood that was slowly being washed away by the rain; life had obviously been extinguished. Racing over to him Kia noticed a young girl standing to one side looking down at the boy.

"He won't get up," the girl told Kia as she approached. "The car hit him and now he won't get up."

"I think he just bumped his head," Kia said, squeezing the girl's shoulder as she passed. "Let me have a look, I'm sure he's fine. Is he your brother?"

The girl nodded. "He's called Peter... but I call him Petey."

"Okay then, you just stay there and I'll check that Petey is all right."

Kneeling down on the sodden ground Kia lay her hands on Peter's chest, there was no movement of breath and no feel of a heartbeat but she knew she could fix that.

The burning in Kia's hand was the most painful she had known so far, she could almost feel the power being pulled from her body and filling his, repairing his injuries and restoring his life. By the time Peter took his first breath Kia was exhausted and she almost fell backwards. His wounds had obviously been far more extensive than they had appeared, but the look of joy on the young girl's face as her brother began to sit up made any discomfort Kia felt unimportant.

"Help me, please..." The distressed voice made Kia struggle to her feet, shaking of her tiredness as she moved around the side of the vehicle.

The passenger's door was crushed inwards and the woman trapped inside looked pale and afraid. A few men were pulling at the door on the other side of the car, trying to free the woman's husband who was face down on the driver's airbag, apparently unconscious.

"Are you hurt?" Kia asked, knowing that an unconscious accident victim was usually a more urgent priority than a conscious one.

"I can't move my leg," the woman said, fear bright in her eyes. "And I think I'm bleeding... my baby..."

For the first time Kia noticed the large bump of pregnancy under the woman's sweater.

"Try not to panic," Kia said, trying to keep her voice calm and them woman's attention on her as the men continued to heave at the driver's door. "Just take my hand and everything will be all right."

This time the pain was less intense but the rush of energy caused Kia to fall to her knees as her strength left her, but she held on tightly until she was sure she had done what she needed, then her grip eased and she fell backwards to the ground.

"Kia are you okay?" Sofia's hands were on Kia's shoulder, helping her friend to sit upright.

"The driver is hurt," Kia said quietly, "I need to get to him."

"Look at you, you're shattered."

"It doesn't matter... please Sof..."

A cheer went up as the driver's door finally gave way and a wail of ambulance sirens could be heard in the distance.

"An ambulance is nearly here K."

"They can't do what I can... you know that."

Sofia knew it was pointless arguing and guided her friend around the car to where the driver's door hung open, the men standing around suddenly unsure of what they should do, one of them commenting on how he was sure you shouldn't move someone in such circumstances.

"Let me through," Kia said, trying to push a particularly large man out of her way, "I'm a nurse." She figured it was only a small lie under the circumstances.

The driver's hand was cold when Kia took hold of it and when she touched his neck there was no hint of a pulse.

Taking a deep breath Kia braced herself for another onslaught of pain but nothing came, she concentrated harder but still nothing. The driver's condition remained unchanged. Using both hands Kia tried again but once more there was no heat, no pain and more importantly, no healing.

As the paramedics arrived and ushered Kia and the rest of the crowd out of the way she felt numb.

"I couldn't do it," Kia said quietly as Sofia led her back towards her mini. "I couldn't help him." The tears that began to roll down her face where hot against her chilled skin but Kia didn't even notice them.

"You're exhausted," Sofia said kindly, "You'd already done more than anyone else could have."

"But it wasn't enough…"

"It has to be."

"His wife is pregnant… that baby is never going to know its father…"

"But that baby is going to live… and that wouldn't have happened without you."

"But what if she wasn't all that hurt? I mean not as badly as he was… if I'd gone to him first then maybe the paramedics would have been able to help her anyway…"

"There's no way you can know that Kia." Sofia bit at her lip, Kia looked so distressed and she had no idea how to help. This was not a situation she was equipped to deal with, nobody was.

"I thought I would be able to help them all... do I have to choose? Am I expected to pick and choose who I save? How do I do that Sof?"

"I don't know K. I really don't."

Kia didn't remember getting home, she assumed that Sofia had driven her but she had no recollection of the journey. She didn't hear her friends say goodbye as they passed her into her mother's care and she didn't register when Katherine eased her down onto the sofa and pressed a hot tea into her hand.

Kia's automatic response made her sip at the drink but she didn't taste it or feel revived by it.

She was completely numb and closed down. Katherine had warned her that the gifts they had were not always as easy to cope with as they might first appear and now Kia felt only too keenly the emotional and physical costs of being a healer and she wasn't sure it was something she could do. It was hard. Too hard.

Xander dropped everything the second he got Katherine's call, she hadn't been able to tell him much for fear that someone could overhear, but the one thing she had been able to say was more than enough. Kia needed him.

Katherine had always been proud of the close bond she shared with her daughter, there was never any question of their trust and faith in each other but for the first time Katherine felt powerless to help. Kia hadn't spoken since Sofia brought her home and Katherine wasn't the sort of foolish person who would continue to insist they were the best person to help when she knew that wasn't the case.

However close the bond between Katherine and Kia it paled in significance to that of Kia and Xander. There was something between them that had possibly never happened before and if anyone could pull Kia out of her stupor then it was the heir of the God Isydro.

Katherine felt a sense of relief when she heard a car pull up outside the house; she had the front door open before Xander even got to it. Not a word passed between them as Xander approached, the grave look on Katherine's face was all Xander needed to know and Katherine stepped back to let him pass, her head indicating Kia's location in the living room.

Xander rushed into the room with such momentum that he virtually threw himself to his knees before Kia, cupping her face in his hands she lifted it to look at him. There was such sorrow in her eyes that Xander could hardly breathe and he instantly understood the pain he had seen on Katherine's face, her gift must have made her daughter's distress unbearable.

"Hey, hey," Xander said in a hushed voice, his lips peppering tiny kisses on Kia's eyes and cheeks as he spoke, "What's the matter? What's happened?"

Kia opened her mouth to speak but no words came out, instead a fresh bout of tears tumbled silently down her cheeks and onto Xander's hands.

Xander turned his head to look at Katherine who was standing in the doorway, her hands twisting around each other as she moved from foot to foot seemingly unable to keep still.

"What?" Xander mouthed to Katherine, his face contorted into a mask of fear and concern, something terrible must have happened to Kia to leave her in such a state.

"I failed..." Kia said, her voice hardly more than a hoarse whisper but it was enough to snap Xander's attention back to her.

"What do you mean failed?" Xander asked, his tone as soft as the gentle fall of snow he had so recently willed into existence to impress her.

"I'm meant to heal... but he died... I tried so hard but I couldn't bring him back..."

"Oh Kia... you can't save everybody, you know that, you told me that..."

"But him I could have... I should have... it was just a car crash, it wasn't his time to die... I didn't know... If I'd known..."

"Known what?"

Kia's voice failed her once again and she grabbed onto Xander's plaid shirt, pulling him close and burying her face in his chest as she wept.

"She ran out of the strength to heal any more," Katherine explained as she stepped closer, desperate to help, to offer her daughter the comfort she so clearly needed and yet she knew she was no longer the person Kia most needed.

"I should have realised," Xander said, shaking his head, his hand gently stroking Kia's hair as he rocked her slowly. "Kia, Kia, this wasn't your fault... you couldn't have known... if only I had thought, it's so obvious now... I wish I had thought sooner and maybe I could have saved you this."

"What do you mean?" Kia sniffled, pulling back from Xander to look at him, her eyes were red and swollen but her distress seemed at least a little lessened by his presence.

"We might be descendants of the Gods, and Goddesses of course, but we're still mostly mortal... they gave us these amazing gifts but they couldn't do anything about our human limitations. The first time I tried to control the weather I nearly killed myself, I tried so hard to create every type of weather I could think of and I drove myself to exhaustion ... my father had to carry me to my bed, I couldn't even stand...because I didn't know my limits. We are not them Kia and we can't do as much as they can."

"But that man died because I..."

"No!" Xander's tone was harsh and Kia stopped dead. "Not because "you" anything! He died because he had a terrible accident, and I am assuming that you had no strength left for him because you had already helped some other people?"

"Well yeah but..."

"There is no but to this Kia... I know you're hurting right now but you have to hold on to the good you did manage to do and not dwell on the times when you can't make everything all right again... you can't save the world and you will drive yourself crazy trying to."

"I just wanted to help," Kia said quietly, the logic of Xander's words were slowly sinking in through the fog of Kia's grief and she grabbed his hands, squeezing them hard as if to reassure herself that the world was still as solid as it had been earlier.

"I know you did my darling girl," Xander said with a smile that lit a spark in Kia's heart, "And you did... you do... and you will carry on doing for the rest of your life, you can't let this one instance damage that."

"Thank you," Kia said, her voice hardly a whisper and her eyes closing as she tried to fight leaden eyelids. "I'm so tired."

"Come on," Xander said as he got to his feet and scooped her up into his arms. "You need some sleep."

Kia was already unconscious by the time Xander laid her in her bed, pulling her duvet up to cover her and pressing a light kiss to her lips.

"Sweet dreams my princess," he said, brushing a few loose strands of hair from Kia's face before leaving her to get the rest she so desperately needed.

"Will she be all right?" Katherine asked as Xander descended the stairs.

"She's exhausted; I think she'll probably sleep for a long time now, I know I did... but she'll be fine."

"Thank you for coming."

"Of course I would come, Kia needed me... and any time she needs me I'll be there for her, nothing is more important."

"She's very lucky to have you."

"Not as lucky as I am."

Chapter Sixteen

Kia shivered, pulling her coat tightly around her as she grappled to get her gloves out of her pocket. The first of the winter snow was threatening to fall at any minute but Kia still had so much shopping to do before she could head home.

No matter how many shops she had been in, Kia couldn't find it, not that she knew what "it" was but somehow she was certain that she would recognise it when she finally saw it. The present, the perfect present for Xander.

Her friends had been easy to shop for, the three of them liked most of the same thing and she had snapped up a selection of presents within the first hour. Katherine was slightly harder as she always insisted that she neither needed nor wanted anything from her daughter. Instruction which Kia ignored every year, usually managing to find something that her mother adored and this year's silver photograph frame would be no exception, especially when Kia made a copy of an old battered photograph of the two of them to slip inside it.

It was one of Kia's favourite old photo's showing a young and happy Katherine holding her new baby girl in her arms, Kia was only a few days old but she already had a look of her mother and she showed the true contentment of a babe in arms.

Xander was another matter, despite how close they were; to the extent where they would often spend hours together without speaking and yet still communicating easily with each other. So why couldn't she find him a Christmas present? What was it about Xander Matthews that made him so completely impossible to shop for?

The truth was of course that Xander would have been more than happy with dozens of the gifts Kia had selected and then rejected. They weren't right however; they weren't good enough. They weren't "IT".

Kia's jeans pocket vibrated the arrival of a text message and it took a few minutes of juggling her shopping bags before she managed to get to it.

"You in town?" Xander's message asked.

Kia smiled. Just the sight of his name was enough to make her heart jump and the fact that he asked that question meant that he had finished work early and was looking to meet her.

"Yeah," Kia replied. "Shopping."

"Fancy meeting for a coffee?"

"Make it a hot chocolate and you're on!"

"Giorgio's, five minutes."

"Make it ten, I'll go dump my bags in the car."

"Love you xxx"

Kia almost skipped to her car, the quest for the perfect present temporarily forgotten as she filled the boot with the bags of shopping she had acquired over the past couple of hours, shaking out her arms at the physical relief of having finally put them down.

Xander was already at Giorgio's when Kia arrived, his hand shooting into the air to attract her attention as she walked through the door.

The cafe's owner George, an elderly man who thought that "Giorgio" made his small establishment seem far more appealing despite having never been anywhere near Italy in his life, waved and smiled as Kia walked over to Xander's table.

They were such a lovely young couple George thought with a smile, always so polite and thoughtful, not like some of the rude kids he got in the cafe sometimes. And the way they looked at each other, reminded him of his beloved Judith, god rest her soul.

"Did you get it?" Xander asked as Kia sat down, before leaning forward to kiss her lips, intending a quick peck but unable to resist lingering a little longer. Xander really could not imagine a time in his life when kissing those lips wouldn't give him that same breathless thrill.

"I am not telling you," Kia replied, shrugging off her coat before wrapping her chilled fingers around the hot mug of fluffy chocolate drink.

Kia had made the mistake of mentioning that she was struggling to find a gift for Xander and now he teased her about it at every opportunity.

"You've nothing have you?" Xander said with a twinkle in his eye as he sipped his coffee. The truth was he didn't really care if Kia had found him some amazing present or not, as long as he had her in his life there was nothing else he needed, but that didn't mean he couldn't enjoy teasing her.

"You will find out Christmas day," Kia said confidently before stopping to consider her own words. "I will see you on Christmas day won't I? I mean I know you'll want to be with your folks but... well you will come around to see me... or I can come to yours?"

"Course we'll see each other, to tell the truth Christmas is never much of a big deal to my family, never has been."

"How come?" Kia couldn't imagine such a thing; from her earliest memories Christmas had always been special for her. Katherine had never scrimped on decorations which were strewn throughout the house and even though their family was only small, just the two of them, when Katherine's mother died Christmas day was still filled with fun and laughter, Kia's friends joining them for a party in the early evening which had been known to last through to the early hours of Boxing Day.

"I don't know," Xander said, pursing his lips in consideration and taking a slow sip of his drink. "I suppose it's the whole religious aspect of it... I mean we can hardly see the idea of "god" the same way as most people."

Kia couldn't help but laugh, that thought had never even crossed her mind. Despite the Christmas carols and the school nativity when she was younger Kia had never really made the connection between Christmas and religion. To her, and she realised to Katherine too, Christmas was a celebration of family, friendship and love.

"Do you do anything?" Kia asked, secretly hoping that Xander would say no so that she could have his company for the whole day.

"Well yeah sure," Xander replied, to Kia's slight disappointment. "I mean we exchange some presents in the morning, then for the last few years my father had opened the restaurant for a Christmas lunch... I imagine that's already fully booked, it is most years."

"So after the presents you can come to mine?" Kia asked, the brightness of her smile and the way she bounced in her chair making it a question that was impossible to refuse, had Xander even wanted to.

"I suppose I can fit you in to my busy schedule, if only to get my hands on this amazing gift you have for me!"

Kia curled up her nose and poked her tongue out at Xander in response, causing him to spit half a mouthful of coffee across the table as he burst out laughing, which in turn caused Kia to snort up a nose full of foam from her chocolate which set off a sneezing fit.

"You two kids!" George admonished with an almost grandfatherly smile as he rushed over with a pile of paper napkins to dry off the table, passing a few to Kia as she continued to sneeze. "What are you trying to do!"

"Sorry George," Xander said, still gasping for breath as his laughter finally eased until another violent sneeze from Kia set him off again.

"It's a good thing you're two of my favourite customers, that's all I can say!"

Two days later and Kia had all but given up finding the perfect Christmas present for Xander. She stomped half-heartedly through the shopping precinct, looking in all the windows that she had stared intently into for weeks now in the vain hope that she would spot something this time that she hadn't before.

Every other present she needed was already bought, carefully wrapped and stored at the back of her wardrobe. Every other aspect of Christmas was organised to perfection. Everything was as it should be. Apart from the most important part of all and Kia found herself holding back tears as she passed the jewellers that she had already scoured for ideas.

There was a gorgeous display of elegant men's watches, any one of which would look right on Xander's wrist. Right, but not perfect.

Kia sighed. She might just have to settle for below perfection as she was rapidly running out of time, the more she looked the harder it seemed to find anything let alone that one special thing.

That's when she spotted it; as she began to turn away something caught her eye making her stop and turn back. Kia had looked in that window countless times, she must have seen that display before but it was as if she was seeing it for the first time and her face lit up, her hand slapped on the glass as she leaned forward for a closer look, making sure it really was as perfect as she thought. It was. She'd found it. There was Xander's Christmas present. Kia was inside the shop only seconds later.

***

Katherine sipped her morning coffee seated at the breakfast bar and sighed contentedly. As much as she loved having her daughter's friends around at Christmas she enjoyed the early morning peace before the festivities kicked in. She had felt a little disappointed when Kia had announced that Xander would be joining them for the majority of the day. As much as Katherine liked, by now even loved, the young man there was no denying that she missed the time she used to spend alone with Kia. Her little girl had grown up and Katherine knew that she had to slowly, and a little reluctantly, let her go.

"Hey mum." Kia padded into the kitchen, with her hair sticking up in various directions and wearing her fluffy, teddy bear pyjamas that made her look very much like the little girl Katherine had just been telling herself she no longer was.

"Happy Christmas sweetheart," Katherine said, reaching for Kia, her arm wrapping around the girl's waist as she pulled her into a warm hug. The sleepy scent of Kia so familiar and comforting that Katherine held on to her a little longer.

"Is there any breakfast?" Kia asked between yawns once Katherine had finally let her go.

"What do you fancy?"

"Do we have any hash browns? And scrambled eggs?"

"I think we can manage that. What time is Xander due over?"

"Around twelveish he said."

Katherine smiled to herself as she turned to begin preparing the breakfast. It was only just past eight o'clock, she still had a few hours to spend alone with her daughter to celebrate what she suspected would be the last Christmas morning where it would be just the two of them.

Xander arrived just after mid-day in what was possibly the tackiest Christmas jumper Kia had ever seen. She burst out laughing the second he took his coat off and was still going strong as she followed him into the living room.

As soon as Katherine saw him, try as she might to remain polite, she couldn't hold back the laughter either.

"Nice jumper," Kia gasped, her words struggling to get out amidst her hysterics.

"They're my mother's idea," Xander said with a roll of his eyes. "And if you think it's bad now..." Xander pressed a switch that was fastened to the hem of his jumper and suddenly the gaudy Christmas tree, which was decorated with fluffy baubles and shiny tinsel burst into life with the addition of lots of little flashing lights.

"That is really lovely," Katherine said, her eyes watering slightly as she tried to hold back a fresh bout of laughter.

"Yes, yes, I know, come on... laugh it up. But just you wait," Xander said pointing a finger at Kia. "Next year you're coming to mine in the morning and she'll make you wear one too!"

"I thought your folks didn't really go in for the whole Christmas thing," Kia said as she finally calmed down.

"No they don't," Xander said as he threw himself down on the sofa, one arm outstretched to invite Kia to join him. "But for some unfathomable reason my mother just adores gaudy Christmas jumpers, all the staff in the restaurant are in them today too."

"Well I think they're fun," Katherine said with a grin.

"Do you want me to ask mum to get you one too?"

"No thanks love," Katherine said, watching the little lights dancing on Xander's jumper. "I think I'll pass."

"Don't blame you, I would too if I could!"

"Well I think you look cute," Kia said, giving Xander a kiss as if to prove her point.

"Of course you do," Xander replied, "That's why you nearly wet yourself laughing when you saw it."

"It was... erm... unexpected!"

"At least I can take it off now that I'm here," Xander said, sitting forward so he could finally free himself from the hideous garment.

"Don't you dare!" Kia said, laughing as she pushed him back. "You have to keep it on now that I've seen it... or you won't get your present!"

"So you finally found something did you?"

"Did you ever doubt it?"

"Just promise me one thing Kia…"

"What?"

"It's not a jumper is it?"

Leaping up from her seat Kia grinned as she raced off to her room to get the parcel that was waiting on the middle of her bed, returning breathless and excited mere seconds later.

"Open it and find out," she said holding the parcel out to Xander, her eyes sparkling with pure excitement. It was perfect, she knew it was, and he would love it.

Xander pulled carefully at the purple ribbon threaded around the parcel, the silver holographic paper falling away as it was unfastened. Inside the paper was a deep mahogany coloured box emblazoned with the logo "Rotary".

Xander nodded his approval; this was obviously a watch, and one of considerable quality.

Flipping the box open Xander's eyes widened. Inside was a watch as expected but not any ordinary watch. Rather than a plain watch face it had a photograph of himself and Kia, the slender golden second hand sweeping past their faces as it marked the passing seconds. He remembered that photograph. Kia had sent him a copy of it months ago. She had taken it in the park on their first date, the day of their first kiss that had ignited such a fire between them.

"It's gorgeous," Xander said pulling it from the box to admire in more light. Now whenever he needed to know the time he would get the added bonus of Kia smiling back at him.

"You really like it?"

"No. I love it."

"It's engraved too."

Turning the watch over Xander saw the engraving on its back. A tear formed in the corner of his eye as he read it and he brushed it away quickly.

To count the seconds until I am with you.

"I... I don't know what to say."

"I told you I would find the perfect thing didn't I?"

"And you really did, thank you so much."

Taking off his old battered watch Xander quickly fastened the new one to his wrist, holding it up to admire it a little longer.

"You are welcome," Kia said, clapping her hands in excitement, revelling in the look on his face as he continued to turn his wrist this way and that as he looked at his new watch.

"So?" Kia asked after a few minutes.

"What?"

"Xander!"

"Oh right yes... I think I have a little something in here for you."

Kia's excitement intensified as he pulled a parcel from behind his back, she had no idea how he got it here without her seeing, but she was far more interested in its contents to worry about that.

The multi coloured Christmas paper was held closed by small strips of Santa patterned tape and it took seconds for it to be torn away to reveal a black box, velvet to the touch, which in turn opened up to expose a shimmering diamond necklace.

Kia gasped as she looked at it, almost falling back down on the sofa next to Xander, her eyes wide as she stared into the box.

"Is that real?" While she had no true concept of the value of diamonds she knew that this one, while still small enough not to be gaudy, was large enough to be of considerable expense.

"Of course..."

"It's stunning... really beautiful..."

"No more than you deserve... here..." Fishing the necklace from the box Xander moved onto his knees so that he could fasten the delicate golden chain around Kia's neck, leaning back to admire it.

"It's perfect," Kia said, her voice hushed with awe that someone loved her enough to buy her such an incredible gift, her fingers touching lightly at the diamond.

"Oh and I got this to go with it," Xander said casually, pulling another box from his trouser pocket and flicking it open before Kia could even register what it was.

Her eyes, as wide as they were before, almost doubled in size as she gazed at the item Xander held out before her. A shining golden band that supported a single glimmering diamond.

"Well?" Xander said, taking the ring out of the box and offering it to Kia. "What do you say? Will you marry me?"

Kia flew off the sofa and into Xander's arms causing him to go crashing to the floor, the diamond ring shooting across the room as Kia smothered his face in kisses.

"Is that a yes?" Xander asked his voice singing with laughter and joy.

"What do you think?" Kia said, kissing him even harder as if to emphasise the point.

Watching from the sidelines Katherine bent down to retrieve the ring that had come to rest by her feet. The happiness in the room was almost overwhelming as it surged through her senses, making her whole body tingle with the happy couples emotions, but she couldn't help but fight of a hint of her own sadness.

Her little girl really was no longer her little girl. Kia was a woman now, and soon to be a married woman it seemed.

Kia had known Xander for just a few months, it was too soon, too fast, Katherine thought she should object but at the same time she knew she wouldn't for any objections would not come from concern about the love the couple shared but for her own life without Kia as a daily part of it. It didn't matter if Kia had known Xander five minutes or five years, the bond between them was undeniable and their love the sort that fairy tales were made of.

"I think this is yours," Katherine said holding out her hand, the bright diamond ring resting on her palm.

Taking a careful hold of the ring, after finally getting up off the floor, Xander turned to Kia, his face more solemn than she had ever known it as he took hold of her left hand and slipped the ring onto her finger. It was a perfect fit, somehow there was no doubt that it would be.

The Christmas evening party that year was one of unrivalled fun and celebration and Kia's family and friends joined together to celebrate her engagement to the man she couldn't remember not having known all of her life.

Even Xander's parents, not normally the sort to party, stopped by for the festivities, adding their approval to their son's choice of future wife and welcoming her into their family.

Kia couldn't imagine it was possible to be happier than she was at that moment, her heart was so full she was sure that everyone in the room could feel her emotions, not just those blessed with the gift of empathy.

As the evening wound down Kia found Katherine sitting alone in the kitchen, the room was only illuminated by the light from the adjoining room, causing the woman to be shrouded in shadow.

"Mum? What are you doing in here?" Kia asked, a flash of light darting across the room and over Katherine's face as Kia opened the refrigerator door. "Is everything all right?"

"I just needed a breather," Katherine said, turning her face to smile at her daughter, hints of tiredness showing around her eyes. "It's been quite a day."

"It really has," Kia said, moving to sit beside her mother at the breakfast bar, resting her head on Katherine's shoulder. "I had no idea he was going to propose."

"He loves you very much."

"I know... I love him too... I can't believe how lucky I am to have found him."

"I don't think it was luck," Katherine said with certainty.

"How do you mean?"

"I don't really know... just a feeling I get... but something tells me the two of you, it was meant to be."

"I think you could be right."

"I know I am."

Chapter Seventeen

"Xander it's freezing!" Kia said as she stomped through the snow a few paces behind him, her hands stuffed deep in her pockets and her breath coming out in puffs of white against the dark winter sky.

"Not much further," Xander said, reaching back to take Kia's hand to pull her closer to him.

"Climbing a hill on the edge of town is not how I usually spend my New Year's Eve you know," Kia said through chattering teeth. "Sof and Rebs will be clubbing it by now."

"It'll be worth it.. trust me..."

"I can't believe you've packed a picnic in the middle of winter."

"Are you forgetting who I am?"

"No but you can't... Xand what exactly are you planning?"

"Just wait and see... ah here will be perfect. Hold this." Xander handed Kia the picnic basket he had been carrying, causing her to grunt at the sudden unexpected weight, exactly how much food had he packed in there?

Closing his eyes Xander stretched out his arms, in what Kia thought was a slightly over the top gesture, and in a circle above his head the dark snow filled clouds parted, the bright moonlight shining down on the patch of grass where the snow had already melted away.

Xander grinned as he held out his hand to Kia, a grin that grew even wider as she stepped next to him, gasping at the sudden heat. As if to test what he had done Kia stepped away again and the instant hit of winter cold caused her to shiver violently.

"How?" Kia asked, returning to the pocket of warmth.

"I've been practising, you know how I said changing the weather was exhausting and I could only hold it for a short time, well I realised that if I just focus on an isolated spot then I can hold it for a few hours."

"So we have our own oasis of summer in the middle of winter?"

"Pretty cool eh? Better than some boring club!"

"Can you make the sun shine for us too?"

"Well, no..." Xander said looking up into the deep black of the sky. "It is still the middle of the night, I can't make it day time."

Kia laughed, shaking her head at herself. "I never thought of that... but a summer night for New Year's Eve is pretty amazing."

Kia shrugged off her coat, hat, gloves and scarf as Xander took a large blanket from the picnic basket and laid it on the ground. Kia couldn't believe her eyes as he took out tubs of food from the basket, sandwiches and cakes and the biggest tub of ruby red juicy looking strawberries that made Kia's mouth water at the very sight.

"My father grew them specially," Xander said with a wink as he passed a strawberry to Kia. It tasted even better than it looked and Kia hadn't thought that was possible.

As Kia made herself comfortable on the blanket Xander popped the cork on a bottle of wine, filling two glasses before settling down beside her.

"Cheers," Xander said holding out his glass.

"To an amazing New Year," Kia answered, tapping the rim of her glass against his.

They sipped their wine in silence for a few minutes, their eyes fixed on the scenery below them, the town stretched out with its lights shining in the darkness, as if it had been illuminated just for them.

Despite the volume of food, the pair made short work of it. Before long empty containers were packed back inside the basket, leaving only a few strawberries to linger over. Teasing them against each others lips, combined with the solitude, the wine and the heat caused their temperatures to rise second by second.

As Xander fed a strawberry to Kia he leant forward to share it, the juice running down their chins as the eating of fruit turned into a deep kiss, the sweetness of the strawberries mingling with the sharpness of the wine in a heady mixture as their passion intensified.

Kia shivered as Xander eased her blouse from her shoulders, but it wasn't the cold that made her body tremble, Xander could keep the cold from her in so many ways and she gasped as his teeth sank into her neck causing her toes to curl in pleasure.

Xander was right, this certainly beat going clubbing. Kia didn't doubt that her friends would be having a wonderful time, but nothing could beat the feel of Xander's hands against her bare skin, the taste of his mouth against hers, and shuddering excitement of their bodies becoming once.

"Xander!" Kia's voice was sharp and high pitched as she squealed her fiancé's name, waking him from the light doze he had drifted into. Kia reached for her clothes as a flurry of icy snow fell on her bare skin and the temperature dropped to sub-zero in a second.

"Sorry, sorry..." Xander said, his teeth chattering as he sat upright and refocused his thoughts, the bubble of warmth instantly protecting them once again.

Kia laughed as her urge to dress slowed down, her fingers slowly slipping buttons through their holes. "Well that was quite a wake up," she said with a giggle. "I guess we know you can't control the weather if you're asleep now... unless you're feeling tired?" Kia smile turned into a frown of concern as she checked out Xander's face for signs of exhaustion. As much fun as it was to be in a tropical bubble amidst the winter snow she didn't want him overdoing it.

"A little bit," he replied. "But not from holding the weather." Xander winked as he hooked a finger into the top of Kia's blouse, using it to pull her towards him for a kiss.

"You are a bad man," Kia teased, succumbing to his lips with no desire to resist as the buttons of her blouse began to become undone again.

A sudden flash of light caught Kia's attention and she, rather reluctantly, shrugged off Xander's attentions.

"Oh look," she said pointing towards the town. "It must be midnight already."

As Xander turned to look in the direction of Kia's finger he wrapped his arm around her shoulders, pulling her in close beside him as they watched flashes of light that danced through the sky, the residents of the town celebrating the start of a New Year with the traditional fireworks display.

"It's so pretty from up here," Kia said, "We should do this every New Year."

"No reason we can't," Xander replied. "Oh I almost forgot."

Xander scrabbled over to the picnic basket and pulled out the bottle of champagne and two flutes that he had brought along, intending to pop the cork on the stroke of midnight before getting somewhat distracted.

"Hold these," Xander said passing the two glasses to Kia as he opened the champagne to a satisfying popping sound, the bubbles quickly filling the glasses and spilling over Kia's hands.

"You will never make a decent waiter," Kia teased, shaking the droplets of champagne off her hands as she passed a glass to Xander.

"So my father often said," Xander said with a half smile.

"Happy New Year, Mr. Matthews," Kia said holding up her glass.

"Happy New Year to you, soon to be Mrs. Matthews," Xander said, clinking his glass against Kia's before they both took a sip.

Leaning into each other the couple continued to watch the fire work display as they emptied the bottle of champagne, looking out into the night long after the dancing lights had ended.

"Are you ready for this?" Xander asked when they had finally accepted it was time to leave, the basket packed up and coats and scarves put back on.

Kia nodded, bracing herself for the sudden cold but it was even more shocking than she had anticipated, resembling the sensation of jumping into an icy lake. Kia shivered, slapping her arms around herself to stimulate some heat as the pair quickly made their way back down the hill to the town below.

The combination of alcohol and happiness caused Kia to giggle as she half ran down the hill, she couldn't remember ever feeling quite so perfectly content and could hardly wait to start the New Year; she had a wedding to start planning.

***

"I am sick to death of this cold weather," Kia complained, her gloved hands were shoved deep in her coat pockets but the numbing cold still seemed to gnaw at her fingertips. "When is it summer?"

"Do you want me to make it summertime for you?" Xander asked with a slight chattering of his teeth. His cheeks were flushed pink from the biting cold and it reminded Kia of the night they first met. He had looked so adorable that night when he blushingly tried to chat her up. Now when she looked at him Kia didn't see the cute boy who stammered through his words but rather a beautifully handsome man who made her heart flutter by simply looking at her, as he was doing at that moment.

Pulling one gloved hand from her pocket Kia rubbed at her ice cube of a nose. "Yes please," she said with a pout. She had never been the sort of person who enjoyed the cold weather, but this winter felt as if it had been more biting than usual and, as January neared its end, it showed no signs of letting up.

"Okay then." Xander began to slowly raise his arms.

Kia squealed, grabbing his arms and slamming them back by his sides causing an elderly man who was walking slowly past them, carefully measuring each footstep on the icy ground, to stop and give them a disapproving look.

"Xander don't you dare."

"But you said you wanted summer."

"I do… but if you go changing the season in the middle of the street like that you'll cause a riot… not to mention with that much snow and ice around here the place would probably flood."

"Well don't say I didn't offer," Xander said a little smugly. "You know you only have to say the word and you can have summer all year long."

"In thirty minute intervals maybe," Kia teased reminding Xander that his ability to control the weather had its limitations.

"Yeah fair enough," he conceded. "How about we have a picnic in the garden tonight instead?"

"Now that I do like the sound of."

Since New Years Eve the couple had enjoyed many such night-time excursions, basking in the warmth of Xander's summer bubble where the winter cold was banned.

"I do still wish it was summer though," Kia said again, linking her arm through Xander's and they continued their walk. "And not just for the weather."

"Oh? You have something to look forward to this summer do you?" Xander asked with a playful nudge.

"Nothing much," Kia giggled, "Just thought I might marry this guy I know!"

"Ah he must be quite something if you want to marry him."

"Well he's not that bad... not too hard on the eyes I suppose..."

"I heard he is incredibly hot!"

"Nah I wouldn't say that." Kia laughed as Xander stuck out his bottom lip in a pout. "I would say he was the most gorgeous man in the whole universe."

"Better," Xander said leaning in to kiss Kia's icy lips. "Brr you are frozen!"

"I know... now come on. If we don't get a decision on these wedding invitations we're going to be the only people there."

"Works for me."

Kia laughed. "Me too… but I don't think our mothers would ever forgive us."

"Very true," Xander agreed. "Onwards we go."

Taking a step away from Kia, his feet slipping slightly on the icy pavement, Xander flung his arms out wide. "We shall battle the demons of wedding planning for we cannot disappoint the mothers."

"Xander stop messing about," Kia said, the sternness of her voice undermined by the small giggle as she spoke. "And be careful."

"I am in complete control my love," Xander announced, his feet sliding under him as he attempted an icy pirouette. "See," he said as he came to a wobbly stop. "Nothing to worry about."

"Show off," Kia said good-naturedly, "Now come on and stop playing the fool, I don't want to be out in this cold any longer than I have to be."

"As my lady commands," Xander said, sweeping a low bow as Kia drew level with him causing her to laugh and shake her head at him while she walked past.

With a laugh Xander righted himself and took a step forward to follow her but his foot connected with a particularly icy patch on the edge of the pavement and he lost his footing. Xander's laughter at his own clumsiness stopped quickly when he realised he wasn't managing to stop himself from falling. Kia stopped and turned back the second she heard the laughter go from Xander's voice just in time to see the man tumble gracelessly into the road, directly into the path of an oncoming car.

The car, while going within the speed limit, was still going too quickly for the icy conditions and despite slamming on the breaks the moment he saw Xander falling, the driver did not stop in time.

Xander's cries stopped abruptly as his body connected with the front of the car and he was propelled across the road before coming to a rest. He lay still, too still.

Kia could hear screaming and it took a few seconds to realise that the terrible noise was coming from her own mouth. Even from the other side of the road she could see the blood slowly trickling from the edge of Xander's mouth and the sight was as painful to her as a knife to the heart.

Kia stood frozen to the spot, unable to move, unable to breathe until finally her instincts kicked in.

Xander was hurt, possibly badly hurt, but it didn't matter, it was all right because Kia was there. She could make it all right.

A few well meaning people tried to prevent Kia from crossing the road, they could see the distress she was in and didn't think it would do her any good to get any closer to the poor man lying on the ground, motionless amidst the ice and snow. Kia knew better though and she shrugged their hands away, moving carefully but quickly to Xander's side.

"It's okay Xand," Kia said as she knelt in the snow beside him, her jeans instantly becoming soaked by icy water but Kia didn't feel a thing, her entire focus was on Xander. "You'll be okay, I'm here… you know you'll be okay."

Xander's eyes were open, staring unblinking and unseeing at the sky and Kia tried not to focus on what that meant. The blood coming from his mouth had stopped trickling and was now a red smear that ran down to form a startlingly bright stain against the brilliant white snow.

"I told you to be careful didn't I? If we are going to get married Alexander Matthews you are going to have to start listening to me sometimes."

"The ambulance is coming love, there's nothing you can do for him." Kia looked up at the kindly voice as the middle-aged woman lay a gentle hand on her shoulder. Kia knew she meant well, but she didn't know how wrong she was, she didn't know who Kia was.

"If you didn't want to pick out invitations you should have said," Kia said as she turned her attention back to Xander, her hands stroking the hair away from his face before she took some deep steadying breaths.

Closing her eyes for a second Kia placed her hands on Xander's chest, she tried to ignore how still it felt and how much the lack of a heartbeat chilled her far more than the snow ever had.

The mark on Kia's palm blazed into life, sending an intense pain shooting through her body that made her gasp in shock. Her whole body trembled as she pressed her hands onto Xander's chest, so hard she almost feared she would break his rib, she could hear the wail of the ambulance in the distance growing louder by the second but Xander didn't need an ambulance. He had Kia; he only needed Kia.

Despite the cold a film of sweat broke out on Kia's brow and her breath was coming in ragged gasps as if she had just run a marathon, her body felt as if it had, she was on the edge of physical and mental exhaustion but she couldn't stop. He hadn't taken a breath yet, she couldn't feel his heart beating in his chest and his eyes still stared unblinking into the sky.

"Come on love, the ambulance is here now, let the paramedics look at him." The middle aged woman tried to move Kia out of the way but the intense look in Kia's eyes as her head snapped back to look at her caused the woman to step back, there was a hint of madness there.

"No!" Kia said, her lips curling in a snarl. "I have to help him."

Strong hands gripped Kia's shoulders and all but lifted her out of the way. Once the physical contact with Xander was broken Kia staggered back into an exhausted heap but she still reached out to him, she had to get back to him.

"I'm sorry love," one of the paramedics said kindly after checking Xander's vital signs. "There's nothing you can do for him now."

"I have to help him." Kia's words were breathed rather than spoken, any strength she had was gone and as she saw the paramedic stroke his hands over Xander's eyes, closing them forever, she collapsed into the snow. She was beaten.

Kia was not aware of being lifted into an ambulance; the wail of its sirens went unheard by her as did the questions of the doctor. Lights were shone into her eyes but she did not see them. Katherine, who was contacted by the nurses once they had found Kia's mobile phone in her coat pocket, raced to her side but even her mother's embrace went unfelt. It was as if Kia was no longer there.

There was nothing medically wrong with Kia and in the end the doctors could do nothing but send her home into Katherine's care with the diagnosis of "shock" and the assurances that she would eventually "snap out of it."

After three days Kia showed no signs of snapping out of it. She existed purely on autopilot. If Katherine placed a drink in Kia's hands she drank it, if food was put to her lips she ate it and when exhaustion took hold she slept.

Katherine had never felt so powerless and so helpless in her life. Several times a day she would sit quietly holding her daughter's hand in the vain hope that she would feel something of what Kia was feeling. Kia's grief and pain Katherine could have coped with, she could have understood, but the lack of anything was chilling. It was as if Kia were an empty shell, she had ceased to live the second Xander had gone and the more time passed the more Katherine feared her little girl would be lost forever.

"Kia sweetheart," Katherine said on the fifth day following Xander's death, trying to keep up the notion of a conversation despite Kia's lack of contribution. "Xander's father brought this for you, he thought you should have it."

Taking Kia's right hand Katherine put Xander's watch into it. The smiling image of the happy couple on the watch face seemed a cruel reminder of what was lost but Katherine hoped that in time the memento of the man she loved would be of some comfort to Kia.

The sudden scream was so loud and filled with grief stricken rage that Katherine stepped back in fear as Kia raised her hand and threw the watch hard against the wall, its glass shattering and shards scattering around it as it came to rest, face down, on the carpet.

Kia's screams continued, growing more and more hysterical until they finally gave way into heart wrenching sobs of ultimate loss.

Katherine flew to Kia's side, pulling the girl into her arms and holding her tightly despite Kia's initial resistance. Where earlier there had been nothing now Katherine could feel the extent of Kia's pain and it was all she could do not to howl along with her daughter at such unimaginable loss.

After an hour Kia's weeping eased, her eyes were red and swollen as she clung to her mother for support unsure of how she was supposed to carry on. What was the point of another day now? How could he no longer be there?

"I couldn't save him," Kia said quietly, her voice in the croak of someone who had not spoken for a few days.

"I know," Katherine said, stroking Kia's unwashed hair as she rocked the girl gently.

"I couldn't save him," Kia repeated a little more firmly. "Why couldn't I save him?"

"I don't know sweetheart, I guess...."

"I mean what is the point of having this "gift" if I can't even save the one person I would want to most in the whole world?" In a flash Kia's grief turned to anger, her eyes flashed in fury as she pulled away from her mother's embrace, her voice turning into a fierce snarl. "What is the point of ME if I can't even do that?"

"Kia please, don't," Katherine said as Kia got to her feet, spinning around the room as if looking for something to take her anger out on.

"Tell me why I couldn't save him," Kia shouted, picking up a vase from the mantle piece and throwing it hard against the wall, the shattering sound giving her some small satisfaction. "Tell me why not him?"

"Kia stop it!" Katherine shouted, grabbing Kia's shoulders and shaking her.

"It's not right!" Kia screamed, fighting her mother's grip to find something else to destroy, she wanted to destroy the whole world just as her world had been.

"I know, I know," Katherine said, her voice quieter, gentler, as she held onto Kia firmly until the girl finally gave up struggling and sank to her knees, Katherine going to the ground with her, her hold on Kia never loosening.

"I can't bear it," Kia said in a whisper as exhausted tears trickled slowly from her eyes. "Why couldn't I save him mum? Of all the people in the world why not Xand?"

"I don't really know sweetheart... I can only guess it's because he was part of the line of the Gods... our gifts are from the Goddess... perhaps they just aren't compatible."

"But you could read him the first time he was here, you could feel the heart of him... why your gift and not mine?"

"What I do... it's based on the human part of us, I feel the truths of a human heart... I could feel the history of Isydro in Xander but that was all. What you do is pure Goddess, yours imposes the will of the Goddess on a person to heal them... there must have been something of the Gods that rejected that."

"I want him back."

"I know."

"I don't know what to do... what do I do now?"

"You carry on Kia, there is nothing else you can do. Xander will always be with you, in your heart, but you have to let him go."

"I don't want to." Kia buried her face in her mother's sweater and wept. "I don't want to."

Chapter Eighteen

Kia's dress was simple but elegant, in plain black the soft fabric fell in folds at her knee and the scooped neckline at the perfect level to show her diamond necklace. It had taken many hours of shopping to find it and despite the cost Kia planned to never wear it again. In fact, after the funeral, she was unsure whether she wanted to give it to charity or just burn it.

Apart from the necklace the only other piece of jewellery Kia wore was her engagement ring and that was something she never planned to take off for the rest of her life. It marked a moment in her life of perfection and the only man she would ever love. Katherine had assured her that she would find love again when the time came but Kia refused to believe such a thing. To even consider it would be a betrayal of Xander and that could never happen. Never.

"Are you ready?" Sofia asked, squeezing Kia's hand and offering a supportive smile, an action mirrored by Rebekah on the other side.

Kia was grateful for her friends' support. She knew she had sometimes neglected them in favour of spending time with Xander and after the accident she had been unable and then unwilling to talk to anyone, but still here they were when she needed them most and she knew she could never express how much that meant to her.

"No," Kia replied honestly. "I'll never be ready for this... but I guess it's time to go isn't it?"

"The car is here," Katherine said from the doorway, smiling her gratitude to the two girls who stood guard on either side of Kia. "Can you give us a minute please girls?"

With another squeeze of Kia's hands Sofia and Rebekah left the room, exchanging sad smiles with Katherine as they passed.

"How you doing?" Katherine asked, tucking a strand of hair behind Kia's ear.

"I don't really know. I feel like I could throw up at any second... I don't know if I can do this."

"You can. We're all here for you."

"I don't want to do it."

"I know. But you will. Here, I have something for you... I wasn't sure when to give it to you but I think now is the time."

Kia's eyes widened as Katherine reached inside her handbag and pulled out Xander's watch, the glass had been replaced and it showed no evidence of Kia's outrage that had smashed it.

"You got it fixed?"

"I thought one day you would want it."

"Thank you." Kia's eyes filled with tears as she ran her thumb over the engraving on the back, how many seconds would she have to count now before she saw Xander again? With blurred eyes Kia struggled to fasten the watch to her wrist, Katherine finally taking over to secure it in place.

The watch looked oversized on Kia's slender wrist but she didn't care. She had never been as grateful to her mother for anything as she was at that moment.

"Come on," Katherine said taking Kia's hand, "We have go to now."

Kia hesitated, a wave of nausea washing over her. The thought of stepping through that doorway filled her with dread. If she went, if she said her goodbye to Xander there was no going back, no more hoping it was a terrible dream and pretending he would walk through the door at any moment. Xander would be gone, because he was. He was gone and would not be coming back.

Closing her eyes Kia took a deep breath as she tightened her grip on Katherine's hand and with a small nod of her head she took the first step that would take her to Xander's final journey.

***

Kia's whole body trembled, she gripped onto the edge of the wash basin to steady herself, she had never felt so weak or so washed out. Running some cold water Kia splashed it over her face in an attempt to revive herself.

Kia had managed to last through to the end of the service before rushing out to the ladies room. So many people had paid their tributes to the man she had loved and Xander's father had given such a heartfelt eulogy that Kia thought her heart would break all over again.

"Kia?" Katherine called as she opened the door to the ladies toilets. "Kia are you in here?"

"Yeah I'm here," Kia said, her voice a little shaky, her reflection in the mirror showing just how pale she was.

"Are you all right sweetheart?" Katherine approached her daughter, the concern clear in her eyes as she saw the state Kia was in.

"Yeah I... I just felt odd... had to get out of there..."

"Of course you did... it's understandable. How are you feeling now?"

"I don't know I…" Clamping a hand over her mouth, her eyes widening, Kia turned from the sink and raced into one of the toilet cubicles, throwing herself down on her knees only the briefest second before she began to wretch, heaving until she had nothing left to bring up. Kia's eyes were watering and her brow covered with sweat as she got unsteadily to her feet.

Katherine was instantly at Kia's side, a dampened paper towel mopping at her brow as she tucked the girls hair behind her ear.

"I think we need to get you home," Katherine said.

"No, no I can't… there are people out there… I need to… I need to be here… for Xander."

"Kia you're not well."

"It's nothing, I don't know… probably just stress."

"Are you sure sweetheart?"

"Really mum, I have to do this for him."

"Okay, if you're sure." Katherine raised her hand to Kia's brow, feeling for a temperature, certain that her daughter was getting ill. While a little warm because of her vomiting Katherine detected nothing to be too concerned about so she took Kia's hand and give it a reassuring squeeze.

Katherine hesitated, taking Kia's other hand she held them both firmly and looked into the girl's eyes.

"Are you sure you feel up to this?"

"Mum, yes, I said so… why? What is it?" Kia tilted her head to observe her mother closely; she could see something in Katherine's eyes that made her take pause.

Katherine didn't speak for a couple of minutes, instead she just looked at her daughter, her gift of empathy encompassing the girl and reading her completely.

There were all the usual emotions that made up Kia, Katherine could feel the lingering pain of her loss and the undying love for Xander that would always be held in her heart, the love for her friends and family and every emotion in between that combined together and formed into the soul of Kia. Katherine could also feel something else, something new that she had never felt in her daughter before and it took a while before she could put a name to it.

"Kia?" Katherine said pronouncing the name slowly and thoughtfully.

"Mum what is it?" Katherine's keen observation of her was making Kia nervous and she averted her gaze.. catching a look of her pale reflection in the mirror.

"Kia... I think... is it..."

"Mum what? Tell me."

"I can feel something..."

"What? Come on. What is it?" Looking back at her mother Kia was overcome with a sense of dread. Katherine could feel something terrible she just knew it. "Mum please, tell me."

"Kia is there any chance... I mean... sweetheart... are you pregnant?"

Kia couldn't hold back her laugh as she snorted her derision at such a ludicrous suggestion. There was no way she could be pregnant; it wasn't possible.

"What?" Kia said, shaking her head with a furrowed brow. "No, no of course not... I couldn't be... we were always so careful and..."

Kia stopped speaking as a wonderful memory came to the front of her mind in almost glowing vivid colours. She could see herself clearly with Xander lying together on New Year's Eve, the plan had only been for a picnic, neither of them had expected things to get physical in such an exposed location and packing precautions was the last thing on their minds. But that was just the once, what were the chances that one occasion would be the time it could happen?

"Kia?" Katherine let go of her daughter's hand and put her hand to Kia's face.

"Do you really think I am?"

"I think... maybe... what I can feel, I don't know how to explain it but when I touch you I can feel something more than just you, another conscience."

Kia's mouth curled slowly up into a smile as the possibility of Katherine's words began to sink in. She could be pregnant. At that very moment Xander's child could be growing inside her, a part of the man she loved could still exist.

"A baby?" Kia said quietly, her hand falling down to her belly in an instinctive action of protection.

"A daughter," Katherine said with a smile, reflecting Kia's own growing excitement.

Looking down at her belly Kia caught a glimpse of Xander's face on the watch around her wrist and felt a wrench in her heart. A daughter, a little girl that Xander would never know.

"I'm scared," Kia said quietly. "I don't know if I can do it... not on my own."

Pulling Kia into her arms Katherine squeezed her gently. "Well that's alright," she said, "because you won't have to do it on your own will you?

You've got me… and I think I did a pretty good job of raising you so imagine how well we'll do between us."

"You think?"

"No Kia, I know."

Mother and daughter stood in a warm embrace for another few minutes as they let the idea of a daughter and granddaughter really sink in. On the day that a huge part of Kia's life ended another now seemed to begin.

"Is everything okay?" Sofia asked, peering around the ladies door and spotting Kia and Katherine holding each other before the wash basin. Slowly separating, Kia made an almost indistinguishable shake of her head to Katherine before she stepped towards her friend.

"Yeah everything's fine," Kia said with a small smile. "Things just got a bit much for me."

Sofia smiled kindly. "Of course," she said. "People were just asking where you were… we're ready to leave for the restaurant."

"I'll be right there," Kia said, turning back to her mother as Sofia left the room. "Mum, could you do something for me?"

"Of course sweetheart, what is it?"

"Before you get to the restaurant… would you nip to the shop for me… and get a test? I have to know for sure."

Katherine smiled and nodded, she wanted to know as well.

***

The restaurant looked much as it had the day Xander had taken Kia there on their first date, if it wasn't for the sombre atmosphere and the black ribbons around the candle holders it would have been impossible to tell that the people there had gathered to say a sad farewell.

Xander's father embraced Kia as she arrived, an act taking her completely by surprise as, although the man had always been friendly enough to her, Kia couldn't remember him ever having touched her before.

"I never got the chance to say," Kia said when he finally released her, "Thank you for sending the watch to me. It really means a lot."

"My son would have wanted you to have it," Xander's father said, his eyes darting to Kia's wrist as if checking that she was wearing it and hadn't simply put it away in the back of a drawer. "You meant so much to him."

"And he did to me," Kia said feeling a little exposed under the man's unwavering gaze. "I just wish I could have... you know... helped him."

"I know my dear," Xander's father said with a shrug. "Some things are just not meant to be... I guess it was time for Isydro's line to come to an end... I just wish it hadn't had to be my son." Shaking his head slowly Xander's father wandered off into the kitchen, he had food to prepare, he didn't know what else he could possibly do now.

Wrapping her arms around herself Kia shivered. Xander's father had looked so lost, so vulnerable, she could have offered him some comfort in the form of a grandchild but she had kept silent. She wasn't ready to share that news, not yet.

Katherine arrived not long after her daughter, nodding her head at Kia's questioning look and patting her handbag in confirmation. As one they moved towards the ladies toilets, this was not something that could wait.

The second hand ticked around slowly, sweeping past Xander and Kia's smiling faces to mark the passing of another minute, bringing the three minute wait to an end. It had been three of the longest minutes of Kia's life and she wasn't sure she could bring herself to look at the test stick.

What if it was positive? Could she really be a good mother?

What if it was negative? Could she really cope with the disappointment?

Taking a deep breath Kia steeled herself for whatever news that little stick held as she raised it up slowly from the edge of the sink where it had been resting.

"Well?" Katherine asked after Kia showed no reaction.

Lifting her head, almost as if in slow motion, Kia's eyes welled with tears that tumbled down her cheeks as she blinked.

"Kia? Tell me," Katherine said, fearing that she had raised her daughter's hopes for nothing.

"Mum... I...." Kia's voice trembled as she checked the result again. "You're going to be a grandmother."

Chapter Nineteen

"So where are we going first?" Sofia's eyes sparkled as she hooked her arms with Kia and Rebekah, her steps more like skips as they headed out of the town centre car park.

"Sof," Kia said with a chuckle. "You do know we're going shopping for baby things don't you?"

"You know me K. All shopping is good shopping."

"Can we get you some of those big flowery maternity pants?" Rebekah asked mischievously.

"Why would I want any of those?" Kia asked, her eyebrows raised high as she looked at her friend.

"They look like fun."

"Yeah maybe if you're not the one having to wear them... just because I'm pregnant doesn't mean I have to look a mess."

"Quite right," Sofia said with a nod. "You can be a stylish mum to be can't you."

"I can... oh let's go in here," Kia turned and dragged her friends into a small boutique shop that had absolutely nothing to do with babies. "I'll need something nice to wear after I've had the baby!"

"That's my girl," Sofia said entering the shop behind her friend and instantly picking up a deep red skirt, holding it to her waist in front of a mirror.

"I thought we were shopping for me," Kia said, nodding her approval of Sofia's choice.

"Yeah, but while we're out anyway," Sofia said as she skipped off to the fitting room.

Several carrier bags later the three girls finally found themselves shopping for the items they had planned to, each of them cooing and sighing over the delicately beautiful and tiny items of clothing. Cries of "look at this" and "look how small these shoes are" filling the shop as they struggled to choose between the baby clothes they saw.

Kia picked up a small pink baby-grow with a tiny brown teddy bear on its front and her eyes filled with sudden tears at the lettering stitched below the bear. "My daddy loves me beary much."

"You okay?" Rebekah asked as she turned and noticed the emotion shimmering in Kia's eyes, a few tears trickling down her cheeks as she blinked.

"Yeah, you know. I just…" Kia nodded at the baby-grow and sniffled.

"I know," Rebekah said, slipping her arm around her friend's shoulder, their heads leaning against each other as they both looked at the happy little teddy bear.

"It should be Xand here shopping for baby things with me," Kia said with a heavy hearted sigh.

"I know," Rebekah repeated, not sure what else she could say.

"Not that I don't appreciate you and Sof coming with me… cause I really do… the two of you have been great… It's just…"

"We're not him, it's all right Kia, we do understand. But I hope we're not too bad at being stand-ins."

"Course not," Kia said with a smile as she wiped the tears from her cheeks. "You've been brilliant."

"What am I missing?" Sofia asked as she approached, her hands filled with a selection of tiny dresses, most of them too big for a newborn but far too cute not to pick up. "Oh," she said, putting the clothes down on a display stand as she saw what had caused Kia's upset.

"It's nothing," Kia said putting down the baby-grow with an exaggerated smile. "I'm just being silly... really it's fine."

"Hey," Sofia reprimanded, "You are not being silly! It's got to be hard enough expecting a baby, without..." Sofia let her words fade out but they all followed her train of thought, without doing it alone, without grieving for the baby's father.

"So not that baby-grow then," Kia said pulling herself together.

"How about this one?" Sofia asked, holding up a matching item but with the word mummy instead of daddy.

"No this one," Rebekah said offering a third option which had the word Granny on it.

Kia grinned, the granny one was the winner and she placed it in her basket along with a couple of the dresses Sofia had brought over, well the baby would grow into them before too long.

As her shopping was being bagged up Kia couldn't stop yawning, she had never realised that pregnancy could be so exhausting and although she still had over three months to go she could hardly wait to go beyond pregnant and into motherhood.

With the shopping paid for the three girls decided it was time for a late afternoon treat of a cake and pot of tea and, linking arms again, they headed out onto the main high street.

None of them had noticed the couple walking a few yards before them on the busy street until they heard her cry out as she stumbled over something in her path and crashed heavily to the floor before her partner could catch her.

A crowd quickly gathered around the woman as the man frantically dialled an ambulance on his mobile, the sight of blood at her temple sending him into a frantic panic.

"Please hurry," he was saying to the ambulance despatch as Kia and her friends drew closer. "She's unconscious... no I can't feel a pulse, I think she hit her head really hard..."

Sofia and Rebekah both turned to look at Kia and she felt as if she could read their thoughts, she could help, she could make everything all right for this couple but still she hesitated.

Since the failed attempt at saving Xander's life Kia had not been in a situation where her gift was needed and now that she was she wasn't sure she was up to it any longer. The responsibility seemed a much heavier weight on her shoulders than it ever had before and she had been seriously considering taking the choice her grandmother had once taken and closing off her gift for good.

"Kia, what are you waiting for?" Sofia said in a hushed voice.

"I don't know if I can," Kia replied shakily.

"You know what will happen if you don't," Rebekah said in a firm but kind tone.

"But what if I can't do it?"

"Then at least you tried."

Kia peered through a gap in the crowd and could see the man's terrified eyes and he looked around helplessly, pleading for help that no one could give. No one but Kia that was.

"Excuse me," Kia said as she pushed her way through the watching crowd. "Please, let me through, I can help."

"Are you a nurse?" the man asked as she approached and carefully knelt down beside the prone woman.

"Not exactly," Kia said as she took a few deep breaths to calm herself, her heart was racing wildly and her hand trembled as she laid them on each side of the woman's face. "Please just step back and let me see if I can help." Realising that a crowd of people witnessing her gift was not ideal, Kia sat back on her haunches and looked around at them. "Can you please all just step away, this isn't some kind of street entertainment, give this lady some privacy... if you have no business being here can you just be on your way."

Many of the people looked at each other in embarrassment before shuffling away, casting glances back over their shoulders to see what drama they might be missing.

Turning her attention back to the woman Kia did a quick check for her vital signs and the man had been right, there was no sign of a pulse that she could detect.

"Is she..?" The man chewed at his bottom lip not quite able to fully form the question.

Ignoring him Kia placed her hands on the woman's face once more and, closing her eyes, she let the power of healing flow through her not stopping until she heard a sudden gasp of breath.

"What did you..?" The man began and he moved closer.

Getting to her feet Kia smiled, "She was just unconscious... you should let the paramedics check her out but she should be fine."

Returning to her friends Kia looked back for a moment. The man was stroking his girlfriend's cheek with tenderness and Kia realised that although she could not save her own love in that way she could still help so many others; how could she want to give up such a gift?

Chapter Twenty

The sun felt glorious, that comforting embrace of heat beating down on Kia's face as she raised it to the sky. It was the perfect summer's day.

The air was calm with an occasional breeze that lifted the scent of the flowers tempting Kia to breathe deeper to enjoy fully their fragrance.

She didn't know how long she had been lying in the open field amidst a vast array of beautifully coloured wild flowers but she felt no inclination to move. This was what contentment felt like and she didn't want it to end.

"You can't stay here forever you know."

Kia turned her head slowly in the direction of the voice lying to her right. "I know," she said regretfully, "but just a little longer, please."

His eyes sparkled in the sunlight, that beautiful blue grey that could never seem to make its mind up and when he smiled at Kia the dimple in his right cheek was shown off to its full advantage.

Reaching out his hand across the bed of flowers he took a tight hold of Kia's, his smile fading and growing a little sad. "You know this isn't real."

"But I want it to be... I miss you." Kia felt a tear prickle her eyes as Xander raised himself up on one elbow and looked down on her.

"I'm always with you Kia," he said, tracing a finger over her cheek. "I always will be... but you can't hide away in a dream like this, you know you can't."

"I like the dream better," Kia said, catching Xander's hand and kissing his fingertips lightly. They felt so solid, so real, how could he be an illusion, a memory of the man she loved recalled in perfect detail for her to hold once more.

"The real world isn't so terrible," Xander said with a smile.

"You're not in it," Kia said, a single tear trickling over her cheek only to be kissed away by the warmth of Xander's lips.

Resting his hand lightly on Kia's belly Xander smiled. "A part of me will be soon."

"I wish you were here to share this with me. Really with me, to hold me like you used to, not just this dream."

"I know my love," Xander said, his breath warm against Kia's lips as he spoke. "But you have to do this for me Kia... you have to raise our child with love enough for both of us..."

"I will, I promise."

Kia closed her eyes as Xander's mouth pressed down firmly on hers, his kiss deep and intense, filled with the passion of being so long apart that she felt a physical pain of loss when it stopped.

When Kia opened her eyes he was gone and she was staring at her bedroom ceiling, the memory of the dream kiss still tingling on her lips.

Looking down towards her feet Kia saw the mound of her pregnant belly, the movement of the child within pressing down on her bladder.

"Is that your way of telling mummy it's time to get up?" Kia said as she heaved herself from the bed. Nobody had warned her that the late stages of pregnancy could be quite so uncomfortable and any level of movement would turn into an exhaustive battle.

Passing by her dressing table mirror Kia paused and looked at herself. Her hair was in its usual early morning disarray and her nightshirt was stretched to its limit over her belly. Rubbing her back to ease the aches Kia laughed softly at herself, she felt like an old woman not a girl of eighteen. Looking at herself again Kia shook her head and made a mental correction. Not eighteen, not now.

"Happy birthday Kia," she said to herself as she waddled to the bathroom. What a difference a year had made.

The soothing hot water of the shower cascaded over Kia's body which was already tired despite only being out of bed for ten minutes. The physical toil of pregnancy was hard enough but the dreams of Xander had become more frequent recently and, despite the comfort she got from them, Kia never felt truly rested afterwards. It was almost as if she was really there in that beautiful field with him rather than asleep in her bed.

Wrapping her freshly washed hair up in a towel Kia slipped her arms into her large fleecy dressing gown and headed downstairs, if she knew her mother well, and she did, breakfast should be under way. Kia's stomach growled its approval at such a thought.

"Here she is," Katherine said cheerfully as Kia padded slowly into the kitchen, trying not to frown at the dark rings under her daughter's eyes, but Katherine couldn't help worrying, Kia never looked as if she was sleeping these days and just at a time when she needed all the rest she could get. "Another dream sweetheart?"

"Yeah," Kia yawned widely and hoisted herself onto the seat by the breakfast bar, quickly tucking into the scrambled eggs and toast that Katherine put before her.

"Same as the others?"

"Pretty much," Kia said around a mouthful of eggs. "It just seems so real mum… and then I wake up and… oh I don't know… sometimes I think … no… no never mind." Kia turned her attention back to her food rather than voicing her thoughts.

"What, go on…"

"It's silly."

"When has that ever mattered to me? Come on… sometimes you think what?"

"What if it's not just a dream? What if somehow Xander comes to me … or I go to him… or… oh I don't know… told you it was silly."

"I don't think it's silly."

"No?"

"No… but I do think it's just wishful thinking. Xander's gone sweetheart, you know that."

"I know," Kia shrugged. "Maybe it's just crazy baby hormones or something."

"Maybe." Katherine watched Kia eat for a few minutes in silence as she sipped her own coffee. What Kia was suggesting wasn't possible, it couldn't be. Could it?

Kia sighed loudly as she shifted in her seat, it didn't matter how or where she sat any more because within a few minutes her body would be complaining of discomfort.

"I wish this baby would get a move on," Kia said stroking her bump.

"She'll come when she's ready," Katherine said sympathetically, she remembered how uncomfortable the end weeks of a pregnancy could be. "And I'm afraid that isn't just yet…"

Kia bit down noisily on a piece of toast. "Well it can't happen soon enough."

Katherine laughed as she put down her coffee cup, she was pretty sure that when it finally happened Kia would decide it was just a bit too soon.

Shaking her head Katherine tutted loudly at herself. "I haven't said… happy birthday Kia."

"Thanks mum." Kia smiled. Her birthday wasn't going to be the celebration it had been twelve months ago, and there certainly wouldn't be a night out clubbing with her friends. Not like the night she had met Xander. Was that really only a year ago and she had lost him already. It didn't seem possible she had known him for such a short space of time and yet now her life would always have a void where he should be.

"And I know you said you didn't want anything but…" Katherine took a small package out of one of the kitchen cupboards, it was wrapped in pink paper with silver butterflies and a cream bow on top.

"Mum I told you not to," Kia said, her voice objecting but her hands already reaching for the present. "You've already spent far too much on things for the little one."

"Well if I can't spoil my granddaughter then what's the point of being a grandmother! Besides, this one is for you."

"Thank you," Kia said, stretching out her arms for her mother to come in for an embrace. Katherine kissed her daughter's cheek, and squeezed her tightly.

Once released, Kia quickly ripped open the wrapping paper to find a cream coloured box inside, the box opened to reveal a small silver locket on a chain resting on purple velvet lining.

The front of the locket was engraved with a single word "Love".

"It's beautiful," Kia said, quickly wiping a tear from her cheek.

"Open it up," Katherine said with a nod.

Slipping her thumbnail in the groove on the edge of the locket Kia popped it open, a lump rising in her throat as she looked at the pictures inside. On one half of the locket was Xander's smiling face, just as she always remembered him, and on the other was a sonogram of their baby. "Mum it's..." Kia's words were lost in an emotional sob and Katherine pulled her close for another hug.

"I thought you could put a proper photo of the little one in there when she finally joins us," Katherine said wiping away Kia's tears.

"I will... it's just perfect... thank you."

"I know it's not much but..."

"No... it's wonderful... more than enough."

Kia looked at the pictures in the locket again before snapping it closed and hooking it around her neck where it hung just above her heart.

Once the breakfast dishes were cleared away and mother and daughter were sat comfortably on the living room sofa with daytime TV babbling away in the background Katherine turned to Kia to fulfill her final job in handing on the inheritance of the gifts of the Goddess.

"Kia?"

"Yes mum." Kia's hand was fiddling absentmindedly with her new locket as if touching it made her feel closer to the two people locked inside.

"You know what today is don't you?"

"Well the birthday present was a give away to be honest," Kia said with a laugh.

Katherine rolled her eyes at her daughter's lame joke, chuckling slightly despite herself before getting serious again. "It's a year since your eighteenth," Katherine said, "So it's the day you have to decide."

Kia had all but forgotten the "get out" clause of her gift, the one chance to reject it, to return to being as she was a year before. But Kia wasn't the same person she had been a year before, too much had happened and too much had changed. She couldn't imagine not having the ability to heal now, to ease someone's suffering and to even return someone from an untimely death on occasion. There was no way she would want to give that up, no matter how hard it could be sometimes and no matter that the one time she really needed it her gift was of no use.

"There's no decision to be made," Kia said with absolute certainty. "The healing is a part of me," Kia patted her bump as she spoke, "As much as this little one in here is… and I wouldn't give up either of them."

Katherine nodded, she hadn't expected Kia to have said otherwise but it was her role to ask the question, to give the option. She knew that Kia had made the right decision.

***

The sun was too hot as it beat down on Kia's head and the brightness of its glare was giving her a headache. The flowers in the field looked parched and wilted and the air had an acrid tang to it.

This was not the field where Kia met Xander, where she got to spend a few precious moments with him in her sleep. It couldn't be and yet at the same time it was, but Xander wasn't there and although she tried to deny it to herself Kia knew he wasn't coming. Whatever it was that had given her those times in his presence again had passed, something was telling her it was time to look to the future now.

Kia awoke with a jump, it took a moment for her bleary eyes to focus on her bedside clock which informed her it was barely past two in the morning. Then a crippling pain tore through her abdomen and she realised what it was that woke her.

Three weeks after Kia's own birthday and she was about to become a mother.

Hauling herself out of the bed, a slow and painful process which had been difficult enough lately even without the added pressure of labour pains, Kia began to call for her mother.

Gripping onto the edge of her door Kia screamed loudly, the sound cut short as she felt warm liquid suddenly covering her feet. Her water had broke. It was time.

"Mum. MUM!" Kia yelled as loudly as she could, her voice on the edge of panic before her mother's bedroom door opened.

Katherine only had to take the briefest look at Kia to know what was required of her, pulling on jogging pants and a jumper Katherine took a deep breath, although her heart was racing she knew she had to keep calm for Kia's sake.

"Okay Kia calm down," Katherine said, one hand resting on Kia's shoulder while the other massaged the bottom of Kia's back. "This is only the start of things, we've got a while to go yet."

"But it hurts," Kia said, her eyes wide with pain and fear.

"I know sweetheart but you'll be all right."

"You promise?"

"Of course I do. Now why don't you go and get changed," Katherine said looking down at her daughter's stained nightdress. "I'll go and phone the midwife."

"Don't be long," Kia said as she turned to shuffle slowly back to her bedroom where the simple cotton maternity dress was hanging on the back of her door, chosen especially for this occasion.

Dropping her stained nightdress to the floor Kia took the maternity dress off its hanger. She remembered being told that hot water could soothe the initial discomfort of labour pains and a shower suddenly felt very appealing.

Katherine hung up the phone, her face set with determination. She knew exactly what she had to do, Kia's hospital bag was packed and ready and now it was just a matter of waiting for the right time.

"Kia are you changed?" Katherine shouted as she headed back up the stairs.

"In the shower," Kia called back through the open bathroom door, deciding it would be best left open in case of any emergency.

"Take your time, we can't leave for the hospital until your contractions are about five minutes apart."

"But I haven't been timing them."

"Don't worry we can start from the next one."

***

It seemed to take no time at all before the stopwatch on Kia's mobile confirmed that her contractions had grown frequent enough for them to be ready to leave for the hospital.

"Are you ready?" Katherine asked as she fastened the seatbelt around Kia's middle.

"No," Kia replied honestly, she couldn't remember ever feeling quite so unprepared for anything in her life. "Is it too late to change my mind?"

"I'm afraid so sweetheart... I think that little girl is ready to meet her mummy."

"And her granny!"

"Grandmother," Katherine corrected with a laugh.

"Nanny!"

"Grandma."

"Grammy."

"Grand-mama." Both women laughed as the car pulled away from the kerb and set off toward the hospital, a journey which would, according to several test runs, take no more than fifteen minutes.

Closing her eyes Kia began panting heavily like they had taught in the antenatal classes. The pain was beyond anything she had experienced and the thought that it would only get worse before it was over was terrifying. Kia wasn't sure she could handle it, she wasn't sure she would be able to cope, she was sure however that she didn't have any choice at this point. The baby was ready to join the world and there was no stopping her.

"I'm not ready for this mum," Kia panted, her knuckles white as she gripped the edges of her seat. "It's too soon... can she not wait a little longer?"

"I'm afraid not, but you can do this Kia, I know you can."

"I'm so scared."

"I know sweetheart but just you wait till you hold that little girl in your arms for the first time, you'll forget all of this the second you lay eyes on her I promise you. It's like nothing you can imagine." Katherine turned to look at Kia briefly, she could still remember that first moment Kia lay in her arms, her wide eyes staring up at Katherine. She was so small and so perfect that Katherine thought her heart might explode with the level of love that had welled up inside it, and nineteen years later that love hadn't lessened. Now her little girl was going to feel that love for herself.

By the time they arrived at the hospital Kia's contractions had grown in frequency and it wasn't long before she was being told her baby was about to make its appearance.

"Mum, have you got it?"

Opening the side pocket of the overnight bag Katherine pulled out the Goddess pendant and placed it in Kia's hand. Katherine had taken comfort and strength from the pendant on the day she gave birth and she hoped that Kia would find the same.

With one hand holding tightly to the pendant and the other to Katherine's hand Kia began to push, her breathing was heavy as she closed her eyes silently wishing that Xander was there by her side. The pendant seemed to grow hot in Kia's grasp and as it did, her pain eased and she felt a presence beside her that took away her fear and filled her with hope and excitement.

At just before five thirty in the morning the midwife urged Kia to give one last push. Looking at her mother, Kia gritted her teeth, she was exhausted but she knew she had to carry on and introduce Xander's baby to the world.

"Here comes the baby," the midwife said encouragingly. "Just a little more... here we go..."

A moment of silence was followed by the welcome sounds of a baby's first cries.

"Congratulations mummy," the midwife said placing the new baby in Kia's arms. "You have a beautiful healthy little boy."

Kia and Katherine looked at each other, confusion on both of their faces as they returned their gaze to the baby. There was no mistaking that the child in Kia's arms was a boy.

"A son?" Kia said quietly, the fingertips of her right hand touching gently at his cheek, his nose, his arm. He was real, he was there and she could hardly contain the intense rush of emotions that she felt. The baby was mere seconds old and yet Kia knew she would do anything in the world to protect him. She would die for him, she would kill for him, she would bring the world to its knees if it came to that. Most of all she would love him, enough for two parents.

"You've got a son?" Katherine said as she looked down on her perfect little grandchild.

"How?" Kia asked, kissing the top of his head softly.

"Did the scans suggest a girl?" the midwife asked kindly, "They can't always be certain you know."

"I never asked to be told," Kia said. "I just assumed…"

The midwife smiled, shaking her head good-naturedly, she had met many parents who believed they knew the sex of their child for countless reasons, it wasn't the first time she had seen the surprised looks on faces when they were proved wrong. "Well I've been a midwife for a long time now and I can assure you that that's a lovely little lad you've got there."

"Do you think we can exchange all those baby-grows and dresses?" Kia asked with a laugh.

"We'll worry about that tomorrow," Katherine replied, holding out her arms. "But right now I wouldn't mind getting a hold of my grandson."

***

The new baby lay sleeping contentedly in his small cot beside Kia's bed. Tired and sore Kia couldn't be happier, even the loss of Xander had transformed into a bearable pain now that she had her son to care for and she couldn't keep her eyes off him, having to fight the urge to pick him up. Katherine had laughingly told Kia that before long she would be praying her son would sleep as peacefully as he currently was.

"So," Katherine said in the hushed tone that people used around sleeping babies, "What are you going to call him?"

Kia leaned over to look into the cot again, she had thought of so many names over the months but of course they had all been for girls and none of them had a male equivalent that she liked.

The baby stirred slightly in his sleep and Kia couldn't resist placing a finger against his palm where it instantly curled to grip, surprisingly tightly, onto her. Even at only a few hours old she could already see a look of Xander in him, she was sure he was going to grow into a handsome young man, just like his father.

"Do you think it would be wrong," Kia began hesitantly, "I mean do you think anyone would mind... or is it just a bit lame to..."

"You want to call him Xander?"

"Do you think I shouldn't?"

"I think he is your son and you should name him whatever you think is right." Katherine said with a tired smile as she got up from where she was perched on the edge of Kia's bed to take another look into the cot. She couldn't imagine ever growing tired of that little boy's sleeping face. A small tuft of brown black hair seemed to stand up on end on top of the baby's head, despite Kia's gentle attempts to smooth it down, and long eyelashes fanned out on his rounded pink cheeks as he slept.

"I think I..." Kia paused, even before she had asked the question she had known what she wanted to do and the more she looked at the boy the more certain she was that his name was decided. "Alexander Matthew," Kia said finally with a decided nod. "Alexander Matthew Deering."

"Oh not Xander then?" Katherine asked.

"No," Kia shook her head. "That would be too hard, to say his name every day, to hear it would hurt too much... it's still too raw. I will never forget Xander but at the same time I don't think I could bear to be reminded of what I lost."

"Alexander it is then... it's perfect," Katherine said, stroking baby Alexander's cheek lightly unable to resist the desire to touch him but also not wanting to disturb his peaceful sleep.

"Just like he is... Xand would have been so proud."

"I'm sure he is...somewhere."

"I hope so... I wish he could have met our son though... I wish he could have known."

"I know sweetheart... but we'll make sure this little lad knows how much he's loved, and how much his daddy would have loved him too."

Kia awoke after the deepest sleep she had had in a very long time, as soon as her eyes were open her head turned to the cot beside her and her heart leapt in shock when she saw it was empty.

Her head snapped around as she sat bolt upright in bed, despite the discomfort of such a sudden movement, and let out a sigh of relief as she saw Katherine in a chair on the other side of the bed with the baby resting quietly in her arms.

"Mum!" Kia said in a half reprimanding tone, "You gave me a fright; I didn't know where he was."

"Sorry love," Katherine said, not sounding very sorry at all as she rocked the baby, "He was starting to fuss and I didn't want you disturbed, you needed some rest."

"So do you," Kia said as she noticed just how exhausted Katherine was looking. "You've been up for hours, you should get off home and get some sleep, I think we'll both be lacking in that soon enough."

"I'll go soon," Katherine said, getting to her feet and returning the baby to his cot. "Not just yet."

"Mum?" Kia said once Alexander was settled again.

"Yes sweetheart?"

"What do you think it means... me having a boy?"

"I'm not sure... it's never happened before... something to do with Xander's side I suppose..."

"But how will it work now?"

"Work?"

"Yeah, you know... the gifts and stuff... does my son still get that? Do I give him the pendant on his eighteenth? Will he inherit a gift from the Goddess... or something from the God? What I am supposed to do?"

Stifling a yawn Katherine considered the question. Such a thing had never happened before and there was no rule book to tell them what to do next, but at least they had eighteen years to work it out.

"I really don't know," Katherine said with a shrug. "I don't know if he will inherit from the Goddess or not."

"No. I'm afraid he won't."

The two women jumped at the sudden unexpected voice in the room, neither of them had heard anyone enter and yet there she was standing beside the cot.

They knew who she was instantly. It wasn't just the beauty that they had heard described in detail, her dark ebony locks and deep mysterious eyes, or the way she seemed to glow without emanating any actual light or even how her feet didn't actually appear to be making contact with the floor. The recognition seemed to come from a far more instinctual level, some kind of genetic recognition the moment they laid their eyes on her and although they knew her name neither woman felt able to utter it even as it echoed in their minds "Assaie".

Alexander began to stir in his cot, a grumbling sound that was a preamble to crying. Assaie moved to the side of the cot, her lips curled in a soft smile as she looked down on the boy and touched his cheek gently. Alexander instantly settled back into a peaceful and contented sleep.

"He's quite beautiful," Assaie said turning her attention to Kia. "He's going to make you very proud I just know it."

Kia blinked slowly as her mind tried to assimilate the information it seemed to be gathering. Assaie was talking to her, Assaie the Goddess. She was there beside Kia's son. It seemed both impossible and yet perfectly natural.

Kia looked at her son and then back to the Goddess as she remembered Assaie's first words and her love for Alexander helped her find her voice.

"You said he won't inherit a gift?" Kia said, stumbling slightly over her words, the feeling of awe threatening to overwhelm her.

"No," Assaie said with a small shake of her head. "I'm afraid he won't."

"Will he get something from…"

"Isydro?" Assaie said, voicing the name that Kia had been hesitant to say in the presence of the Goddess. "No I don't believe he will inherit from the God either. Your son is... unique."

"How do you mean unique?" Katherine asked, finally feeling able to speak and yet flushing pinkly when Assaie turned to look at her.

"Your grandson is... he is the end of my line... the combination of Goddess and God means that he is both and so neither... as such he marks the end of Isydro's line as well."

"I'm sorry," Kia said, suddenly feeling a rush of guilt that she had been the cause of ending the line of the Goddess that had continued for generations.

"Oh no you misunderstand my daughter," Assaie said with a smile that was more comforting than the warmest embrace either woman had ever known. "Your son's birth is not something to apologise for. The end of my line is not to be mourned but rather it is to be celebrated."

"I don't understand," Kia said with a confused frown.

"For countless generations now I have watched over my daughters, guided them and loved them, as I have with both of you... but this world has long since forgotten about the Goddesses who they once loved, we have not been needed by the people for so long and my sisters grew weary of a world that no longer knew them so they moved on to the next realm."

"But you stayed?"

"I had my daughters to care for, to gift and to watch over... how could I leave?"

"And now you can go?"

Assaie nodded as she moved back to Alexander's cot. "My gifts are done," she said a little sadly. "This beautiful boy could not receive them for they were only ever attuned to my daughter's, but even if you had borne a girl a part of her would still have been of Isydro and would not be able to accept my gift. He is the sign that I can finally join my sisters. I have been waiting for him for so long."

Kia nodded her understanding, her eye suddenly catching sight of the Goddess pendant on the bedside table where she had placed it shortly after giving birth. Taking it in her hand she held it out to Assaie.

"I think this belongs to you."

Assaie smiled at the sight of the familiar object.

"My pendant," she said with obvious joy. "I remember leaving this with Jacob, I had so little time but I knew I must leave my daughter's with something so I charged the pendant with my gifts before putting it in Jacob's safe keeping. It has served us well."

Assaie reached out to take the pendant, although her hands touched Kia's as the necklace was exchanged Kia felt nothing but a slight breath of air as if Assaie were made of nothing at all, yet the pendant sat firmly in her grip before she fastened it around her neck, the figurine seeming to glow as soon as it was back where it belonged.

"So my son is the end?" Kia said looking at the sleeping baby and realising that she would never have to press the pendant into his hand to awaken a part of him that had been hidden. Alexander would always be a whole person, his future purely of his own making.

"He is the end," Assaie agreed. "And he is the beginning... He is a new start and he has the whole world before him."

"Do I tell him of you?"

"If you desire... he should be proud that he comes from a great line, from both his mother and father's sides... and he can still achieve great things even without the gifts his parents received."

"Assaie?" Katherine said, saying the name aloud, which was both exciting and a little frightening.

"What is it my daughter?"

"Why did you come here today? There have been so many generations of us, why come back today?"

"Is that not obvious? To say goodbye, to my line, to the world. To stand for one more time in the world that once birthed my Jacob before I move on."

Katherine nodded, she felt sadness that Assaie would no longer be there to watch over them and yet she saw in the Goddess's eyes her need to make that move into the next realm.

"Thank you," Katherine said softly, not completely sure what exactly she was thanking Assaie for; for visiting them, for watching over them, for blessing them with their gifts or for simply loving them.

Looking down on Alexander one last time Assaie leaned into the cot and brushed her lips across his cheek. The child stirred briefly, his small arms stretching out before him before curling back into a sleep that was made serene by the kiss of the Goddess.

Assaie smiled for a moment, her face turned towards a seemingly empty corner of the room, nodding her acknowledgement to a shadowy male figure and Isydro nodded back.

Kia turned to follow Assaie's gaze but could see nothing, however the Goddess's lips moved in silent conversation and Kia had a feeling the other half of her son's ancestry had come to say his farewells.

"I will miss seeing this boy grow," Isydro said, stepping forward to run a fingertip over the arm of the sleeping baby. "But it is time."

"He will not need us," Assaie said, her eyes flicking towards the two women in the room, "We raised strong children, they will continue to thrive when we are gone."

"Then we must say farewell to this world at last." Assaie took a hold of Isydro's outstretched hand as they both took one final look at the sleeping boy, their past was finally healed and they could both move on.

In no more than the blink of an eye the Goddess and God had gone and Katherine and Kia looked at each other silently for some time, finding it impossible to give words to what they had experienced. Finally Katherine climbed onto the bed beside her daughter and the two embraced realising that there was no need for words.

Chapter Twenty One

Assaie was weary. She had watched over her descendants for so many generations and never once regretted her decision to stay when her sisters had moved on but she was finally ready to join them. The world below her had changed and the love for the three Goddesses had long since faded. Human kind had lost their belief in the Goddesses and Gods who had once watched over them, instead they had founded their own religions and it saddened Assaie that the world had learned nothing from the wars her ancestors had fought as the people of earth now raged wars in the name of their new Gods.

From the moment of Kia's birth Assaie had known there was something special about the girl, although she hadn't known what it would be at the time she had known enough to realise that Kia was one of the few who could take the gift she had blessed her own daughter with.

As Kia had grown, Assaie had seen the girl fulfill her promise but she had still been surprised when Kia had fallen in love with the son of Isydro, and yet it seemed fitting that the descendants of them both should finally unite in such a way.

"Take care my daughters... and my one and only son," Assaie said, her hand pressed against the pendant where it lay over her heart. Closing her eyes Assaie stepped forward and left the heavens for the final time.

When Assaie opened her eyes again her heart sang with joy. Aalegth and Anfare stood together, their arms outstretched waiting to welcome her as she raced into their embrace.

The three sisters held each other for a long time, communicating without words as they basked in the joy of being reunited at last.

"Welcome my sister," Aalegth said as the sisters separated.

"I have missed you both," Assaie said, reaching for her sisters' hands and holding them tightly.

"Was it worth it?" Anfare asked.

"Yes," Assaie said without hesitation. "They were worth it, every second, every century."

It was then that Assaie spotted him, standing some way off but instantly recognisable and her heart skipped a beat.

"Jacob." The name came from Assaie's lips in a breath as she smiled a smile that she had not experienced since the day she had left him.

In Jacob she could see all of his life, the babe she had witness born and the old man whose death she had mourned from the heavens, but mostly she could see the man she had loved. The man she had chosen a mortal life for and the man who had fathered the start of her incredible line.

At Jacob's side stood a woman, her long dark hair and chocolate brown eyes were echoes of the man at her side and the Goddess who observed them. The first of Assaie's line, her daughter Althaia.

Assaie moved forward slowly, savouring each step that took her closer to them as they stood motionless waiting for her.

Another figure was also standing off to one side and when Assaie saw him she hesitated. As much as she longed to return to Jacob's embrace at last there was someone else she had to see.

Assaie's Gift

Turning aside Assaie approached the young man with slightly messy hair and gentle blue grey eyes. He smiled as she got closer and nodded his greeting.

"I am glad to see you here," Assaie said, her hand brushing slowly over his arm. "I was hoping I would... I have just met your son."

Xander's eyes widened in surprise. "I have a son?"

"A beautiful little boy. His mother is very proud."

"Kia... how is she?"

"She mourns you but she has the comfort of your child and she will flourish from now on."

"Will I ever see her again?"

"You will... but she has a long life ahead of her yet."

Xander nodded. It was enough to know that Kia was well and that she had borne him a son, he could wait for her as long as it took now.

Finally Assaie made her way back to Jacob and Althaia. As she got closer she realised it was not just the two of them waiting for her, behind them stood hundreds of women, all of them her descendants, and in that moment Assaie was no longer the Goddess but rather she was a mother, seeing her matriarchy laid before her in countless centuries of daughters and mothers spread out like a woven thread from Althaia all the way down to Katherine's mother. Truly this, more than anything, was Assaie's gift.

Jacob raised his hands to Assaie, which she grasped as soon as she could reach them.

They stood in silent contemplation of each other, drinking in the sight they had both been denied for so long.

"My beautiful Phae," Jacob said at last with a smile that had always melted Assaie's heart. "I've been waiting for you."

A note from the author.

Hello to you, dear reader,

I do hope you enjoyed this little tale of mine. If you did, then please think about posting a review on the site you purchased the book from. There is nothing more wonderful for an author than to get feedback from readers, and as an independent author, those reviews are even more vital.

Please, also feel free to join me on social media where I can let you know about any upcoming projects I have up my sleeve.

www.facebook.com/DEHAuthor

twitter.com/dehauthor

dawndelivers.wordpress.com/

Much love x

About the Author

D E Howard was born and raised in the small seaside town of Southport where she still resides. Enjoying writing for most of her adult life she only recently decided to turn her ideas into books in the hope that other people would enjoy her stories too. Part time gardener (just at home!), part time dog walker (for a crazy cairn terrier) and part time author she still has time for a full time job. Work pays the bills but writing feeds the soul.